HOLY MOLEY, I'M A DEAD DUDE!

HOLY MOLEY, I'M A DEAD DUDE!

C. M. Hopkins

2 Palmer Street, Frome, Somerset BA11 1DS

To Steve Lovering, the coolest dude I know.

Big thanks: Steve Lovering for his contributions, advice and opinions (isn't it time you wrote your own book now?).

To Barry Cunningham for his enthusiasm, support and taste in nutty waistcoats.

To Rosemary Bromley for putting me in touch with Barry.

To Pippa La Quesne for her incisive comments and editing.

To my brothers, Paul Hopkins for making computer know how comprehensive to a technophobe like me and to Dr Steve (Bogus) Hopkins for explaining some of the laws of physics in a language that I could understand (just!) and for his general lunacy.

And finally to: Scott Brenman, a real cool dude.

© The Chicken House 2003
Text © Cathy Hopkins 2003

First published in Great Britain in 2003
The Chicken House
2 Palmer Street
Frome, Somerset BA11 1DS, United Kingdom
E-mail: chickenhouse@doublecluck.com
www.doublecluck.com

Cover design by Robert Walster
Cover illlustration by Will Barras
Typeset by Dorchester Typesetting Group Ltd
Printed and bound in Great Britain

British Library Cataloguing in Publication data available

ISBN 1-903434-86-6

One

'Tonight's the big one,' said Dude, as he pushed his way through a frenzy of fans outside the stadium. 'It's gonna be a night to remember. I can feel it in my bones.'

Tara took his hand. 'Yeah, but let's get inside before this lot get any wilder.'

Dude waved and high fived to the throng of teenagers who were pushing and shoving to get a glimpse of him.

'Rock on!' he shouted, punching the air for emphasis.

'Rock on, Dude, rock on,' the crowd chanted back.

Much to Dude's delight, many of the fans were wearing his band's name and slogan on their T-shirts. Dirty Laundry (we do it in public.) Being recognised was still new to Dude and he wished that Tara shared his excitement but she looked at the crowd warily. The girls looked back at her with undisguised jealousy. Dude sighed. He knew that Tara didn't like all these eager girls going bonkers at the sight of him. He was *her* boyfriend she said and though Dude had no problem with that, these were his fans and Dude wanted to acknowledge them. They'd put him where he was, and he was only just sixteen.

Suddenly, a huge paw landed on Dude's shoulder and he was firmly guided towards the back stage-door by a giant leather clad roadie.

As Dude turned for a final wave, a Goth girl with bright green eyes caught his attention. *Woah, she looks different* he thought. *And she must be sweltering in that get up.* She was wearing a ton of fake tan and was dressed from head to foot in black winter woollies, a fact that might not have been strange if it weren't August with not a cloud in the sky.

When the girl saw that Dude was looking at her, her face lit up and she waved enthusiastically. He was about to wave back when Tara shoved him in past the security guards and slammed the doors shut behind them.

'That girl gives me the creeps,' said Tara. 'I've seen her at a few of your gigs.'

'Really?' said Dude. 'Can't say I've ever noticed her before.'

Once safely inside the dressing-room, Dude went into his pre-gig routine. He'd learnt from the stars, Robbie, Madonna, all the biggies had a good luck ritual.

First he did yoga positions to get himself limbered up. He started with 'the lion' pose which consisted of kneeling on the floor and sticking his tongue out as far as it would go. Then 'the cat' which he did by getting down on all fours then curving his back in the air like an alley-cat. Then, lastly, a position he'd made up himself. He called it 'the dead dog' and it consisted of lying on his back with his arms and legs dangling in the air.

Next, he reached into his rucksack and got out a framed photo of his own personal heroes. A band called Reckless Heart. They used to play at the pub on the corner of his road, and every Sunday when he was back in junior school, he'd sit on the wall outside and listen, vowing to be in a band of his own.

He stood in front of the photo, put his hand on his chest and solemnly said what he always said before a gig. 'Allegiance to the heart.'

Tara stood next to him. 'Allegiance to the heart,' she repeated.

Then as a toast to the success of the night, they each took a slug of Vimto, Dude's favourite drink since he was six years old.

'Right, time for the gunk,' he said plunging his hands into a giant sized tub of hair-gel. Soon he was spiked up, changed into his denims and looking every inch a pop-idol. 'Ready?'

Tara smiled. 'Red hot and ready to rock, Dudemeister.'

Forty minutes later, Dude and the Dirty Laundry were well into the show. It was going brilliantly. Out in front of him, the crowd was pumped up and packed shoulder to shoulder.

As one they chanted, 'Dude, Dude, Dude.' None louder than the serious fans in the mosh pit who bounced, bounded and stomped as Dude cranked things up. At the flick of a finger, the volume lurched from merely brain-battering to a level that would eclipse a Concorde fly-by. Another flick and a cyclone of untamed musical energy shook the stadium to its foundations, thrilling the many armed monster that screamed and beckoned Dude into its embrace.

Now was the moment. His favourite part of the show. Stripping off his guitar, he grabbed the microphone.

'Do you want to see me fly?' he cried.

'Yeaaaah,' they responded. 'Fly, Dude. Fly, Dude. Fly, fly, FLY.'

'DO YOU WANT TO SEE ME FLY?'

'DO IT, DUDE. DO IT. *DO IT*.'

As he'd done at all his gigs before, he took a few steps back, raised his hands high in the air, then ran and dived off the stage into the waiting arms of his beloved fans.

In a flash, he was surfing the crowd. No matter how many times he'd done it, he was always amazed at the speed he was propelled by the thousands of eager hands. *Man what a rush* he thought. *Better than chocolate, better than Christmas, better than his footie team scoring the winning goal.*

'Dude, Dude, Dude,' they chanted as they tossed him deeper into the heart of the crowd. On the stage, the rest of the band began to play a ragged version of the Hawaii 50 theme, the traditional accompaniment when their leader went crowd surfing.

As Dude bounced from hand to hand, the upturned faces blurred below him. He was flying. Up and down. Up and down. *Briiilliant.* Then, in the distance, he caught sight of the woolly clad weirdo. A sudden sway in the crowd and he was going towards her and a gang of her equally strange looking Goth mates. Another lurch from the fans sent him flying into their arms. Over he went, but the hands that reached out to catch him evaporated into thin air. Instead of the support he expected, he plunged right through them as though they were a line of washing.

He was falling, down … down …

His head hit the concrete floor with a *thunk* and the crowd gasped as one, 'Duuuuude. ErrrG?'

He was OK. He was up and flying again. The floor had acted like a super trampoline. *Must be some kind of high tech sport's surface* he thought as he bounced over the crowd again. But no hands touched him this time as he floated up and away. *Er, up and away?* he questioned. *Shouldn't I be going across and sideways?* But no, he was floating up, up and away towards the ceiling of the stadium.

Der, what's happening man? he thought as he came nose-to-nose with one of the house lights positioned on a high beam. *Must have knocked myself out and I'm dreaming.* He looked below. *Hey, weirder and weirder.* Far below him, fans were strangely silent and security men were forming a cordon around some dark haired guy on the floor. *What's happening* he thought? *How did I get up here*?

He saw Tara running. She looked freaked.

'Tara, *Tara*!' he called. 'Hey, what's happening?'

But she didn't hear him.

At the centre of the security men, she was staring at the body on the floor. The band had stopped playing and were standing as though paralysed on the stage. One of the fans began to cry. A lone sob in the silence. Then the wail of a distant ambulance.

'Hey, *guys*!' he called.

But no one heard him.

A sudden tug on his abdomen and Dude felt he was floating again. He melted through the stadium roof. It didn't bother him though, it was kind of nice. *Caramba hoi hey*, he thought, *this is some groovacious dream.*

Above stretched the starry night sky – below the lights of the city streamed towards the horizon. Suddenly, he found himself being pulled into a dark tunnel. At the end was a prick of light and he was heading straight for it. *Coo-ool* he thought as his speed picked up. He felt exhilarated, unafraid. He was an express train racing down the tracks, a rocket streaking through space, and then like a bullet speeding out of a gun barrel, he exploded into a sea of white light.

All was still. Warm. Calm. He felt good, in fact, the best

he'd ever felt in his whole life. Bathed in soft light. He felt gloriously happy, silly, giggly with good vibes.

'I'm on top of the world,' he cried flinging out his arms like Leonardo di Caprio on the stern of the ship in the film, Titanic. He laughed at the thought. *I probably am on top of the world. But what world?* Dude didn't really care, it felt so good, so peaceful. He searched for the words to express exactly how he felt so that he could tell Tara when he woke up.

Then he remembered her, far down below, and how worried she'd looked. *What was happening back there?*

He looked down. It was like looking through a telephoto lens. And then he saw it way off in the distance. Not it. *Him.* Not him. *Himself.* A body. *His* body. He zoomed back through sky, through the roof and back into the stadium for a closer look. No mistake. It *was* him, the Dudemeister, lying there. *This can't be right*, he thought. Then he saw Tara, sobbing, while a paramedic worked frantically on the body.

Suddenly, the paramedic stood up, shook his head and pulled a blanket over Dude's face. *Kind of pale looking* thought Dude, *but clear as day, that was my face. But how can it be when I've been doing just great – chilled out and grooving, on top of the world?*

As the paramedics picked up the stretcher, the audience parted, making a corridor that led to a waiting ambulance outside. No one spoke a word, not even when police-cars arrived. Everyone looked mega freaked.

Tara was in full-flood crying by now and a security man put his arm round her and led her away. Even the boys in the band were tearful.

Dude floated towards his body and Tara.

'Hey, I'm here. I'm cool.'

But she still couldn't hear. Dude looked at the empty shell of his body on the stretcher and the truth finally dawned on him.

Holey Moley, he thought. *I'm a dead Dude.*

Two

OK thought Dude, taking a deep breath. *Let's just chill out and think this thing through. Yes, I seem to be floating fifty feet above the floor OKaayy ... that's cool. But what now* ? he asked himself as he drifted past a massive stage lighting-gantry proclaiming 'DUDE LIVE TONIGHT' in hundreds of light bulbs.

The stadium was empty, the crowd was long gone and the security man had been in and locked up. It was eerie being there all alone and Dude felt scared. *Got to make a plan,* he decided. *Yeah, a plan. But what? Maybe I should follow myself in the ambulance? How bizarre would that be? Where did I go? Must be half a dozen hospitals round here. What do I do?*

As Dude considered his options, he barely noticed that he had floated down through the stage and into the labyrinth of prop-stores and dressing-rooms underneath. Suddenly, he became aware of an overpowering smell of disinfectant as two old ladies carrying mops and buckets bustled through the door.

'Poor kid,' said one nodding towards Dude's poster on a wall. 'He was only a young 'un.'

'Yeah, I know, but that's today's youth for you,' said the other, rustling in her pocket and pulling out a paper wrapped package. 'Blooming tragic. Cheese and pickle or ham, Doreen?'

Dude wafted over to them. 'Er 'scuse me ...'

No reaction.

He tried a little more forcefully adding a cough for emphasis. 'Ahem. 'SCUSE MEEEEEE ladies, pleeease, *talk* to me.'

'Oh ta, Rita. Ham, but best wait till I've done the loos,' said Doreen, taking the proffered sandwich and putting it on a window-ledge. 'Mind you, he shouldn't have been throwing himself about in the crowd like that, asking for trouble he was. Any mustard on it?'

As Rita tucked into her sandwich, Dude realised that he was starving. He floated over to Doreen's sandwich on the ledge and when the ladies' backs were turned, he reached out a hand to pick it up. But his hand went straight through it! *Pants,* he thought. *How am I supposed to eat?* One of his favourite mottos was 'When the going gets tough, the tough have a cheeseburger' so he couldn't imagine life or after life without noshing. How would he survive? *No more sausages, no more chips, no more chocolate.* The thought was unbearable.

'EXCUSE MEEEEEE,' Dude called again.

'No, just ham, love. That OK?"

'Yeah,' said Doreen, picking up her bucket and waddling into the men's toilet, 'But kids today, can't tell them nothing, can you?'

'Too right,' said Rita, through a mouthful of cheese and pickle.

Enough of this, thought Dude, *time for drastic action,* and he tried to grab Rita's arm as she was about to take another bite. He noticed how strongly she smelt of sweet rose talc as he tugged at her but, once again, his hand seemed to be having no effect.

Suddenly, Rita's face froze mid-chew and Dude thought he'd got her attention at last, but no, she was choking on her buttie. She managed a gurgle, then a cough that erupted into a mighty sneeze that launched her false teeth across the room.

Dude ducked the flying choppers, leapt back through the wall behind him and found himself in the Ladies.

Doreen came through a moment later and began mopping like fury. Her mop went straight through him.

'*Oi*', he said stepping out of her way, 'Watch it will you?'

Doreen picked up her bucket and sloshed dirty water in his direction.

'Ee*www*,' cried Dude.

Then Doreen began to sing. 'It's been a hard day's night and I've been working in a bog ...'

Rita came through to join her. 'It's been a hard day's night, I should be sleeping like a frog,' she croaked. She picked up her bucket and with a swing, emptied the dregs right through Dude.

'Guuu*ross*,' he yelped. Then he felt panicky, *sleeping like a frog*? *Don't like this,* he thought. *Maybe I'm caught in a parallel dimension. Sudden blow to the head, happens all the time. Seen it on the telly.*

'Everything's gonna be OK,' Dude said to no one in particular. 'But ... yeah ... had enough now. Thank you very much, enjoyed the floating round and that, but enough, too much of a good thing, wanna wake up now in my own bed, with my own things. All RIGHT?'

He had a last attempt at getting the ladies' attention. He whistled, he hollered, he tried tickling Doreen under her arms but she seemed to be more interested in cleaning a sink.

In the meantime, Rita had started on a Madonna song.

'Like a virgin,' she sang as she danced round her bucket.

'Mopping away the slime …,' giggled Doreen, as she wiped the soap-dispenser.

Utterly exasperated, he shouted, 'Are you two deaf as well as stupid?'

Nothing. So Dude decided to leave the loos and go and see if anyone else was about.

After travelling through endless backstage passages, he found himself up in the auditorium again so he made for the reception at the front. Floor to ceiling glass entrance-doors ran the width of the building so he glided over and peered through a panel into the deserted car park.

What was that? he thought, as he leapt back. Something was out there. A face. Looking back in at him from the darkness. The chubby face grinned and a hand appeared and gave him the thumbs up.

Dude sighed with relief. At *last*, someone could see him. He floated through the door and looked around him. But the face had gone. *Vanished into thin air*, he thought, then wondered if there was such a thing as fat air. His thought was interrupted by the same smiling face and waving hand but this time from *inside* the stadium.

Hey, why not, thought Dude, *it's been a wacko night all round.* So he glided back in through the door again and looked around.

Now the face was outside.

'Stay there,' it mouthed. 'I'm coming in.'

Dude nodded in agreement and watched in amazement as a very plump, grey boy slid through the doors. Amazement turned fast to horror when he realised that the boy was transparent. Dude could clearly see lights from the carpark shining right through his corpulent torso.

'*OhmiiiigoOOOOD*,' cried Dude, turning round and whizzing back into the main hall, down through the stage,

17

through the props-room and back into the Ladies where he hid behind Rita who by now was on a rendition of 'If I Ruled The World.'

The transparent boy chased after him. 'Hey, cool it,' he said. 'No worries. I won't hurt you.'

'No worries? B ... but ... you're a *ghost*,' stuttered Dude.

'Er. Moi? Un ghosto? D'oh?' laughed the boy. 'And what the heckola do you think you are?'

'A musician. You scared me, man,' said Dude, a moment later when he'd calmed down. 'I almost jumped out of my skin.'

'Out of your skin? Out of your ...' laughed the boy, 'That's a good one. As if you had any skin to jump out of. Like it or not, you're a G-H-O-S-T and that spells ghost, brother. Uno dead dude, Dude. So get real, oh sorry ... you can't. OK, get ether-real then. Why does everyone always get so freaked when they see a spook? You don't have a personality change just because you're dead, y'know. You still feel like you, don't you?'

'Yeah. Sort of,' said Dude, after a moment's consideration.

'You don't have any sudden urges to hang about in cemeteries wailing and scaring people?'

'Guess not.'

'No need to pop your eyes out and spin on your head and scare people?'

Dude glanced over at Rita and Doreen who were now leaning up against the wall discussing last night's episode of Neighbours. 'Er, suppose not really.'

'So, cool. Believe me, like in life – which, incidentally, is something you're out of – in *after* life, there are good and bad ghosts, just as there are good and bad people.

It's only people's fear that makes them scared. If they could get over that, they'd realise that some of us can be jolly nice. I'm Grey, by the way.' He offered Dude a podgy see-through hand. 'Sorry I'm late. Hector told me to be here ages ago but … I was at the movies. Um. Don't tell on me, will you?'

'The *movies*? Ghosts go to *movies*?'

'Too right. One of the cools of being a ghoul. You can see what you like. And no one notices us so we can get in without paying. I'll take you. 'Scary Movie 2's' on at the local. It's quite a laugh.'

'And who's Hector?'

'Hector the Spectre,' said Grey. 'You'll meet him soon enough. He's like, um, a policeman. Makes sure we're all behaving and that, you know, stick to the rules.'

'*Rules*? There are *rules* to being a ghost?'

'Yeah, 'course. Loads. Like in life.'

'Like what?'

Grey considered. 'No watching people when they're on the toilet. No hiding in girls' changing rooms waiting for them to get undressed and shower. Stuff like that …'

'Wow,' said Dude, trying to take it all in. 'Weirdosity.'

Now that he'd been talking to Grey, he was beginning to feel better. It was good to have someone to chat to after the wacko night he'd had.

'Hey. Wanna take a look at yourself?' asked Grey.

'Suppose,' said Dude, feeling apprehensive again. He hadn't thought of how he looked. What if he was plump and grey like Grey? Or luminous white with gouged-out eyes and weird wild hair like in the 'Thriller' vid. He'd never seen a ghost before, only the ones in the movies and they all looked yuckocious. He looked down at his feet. They were still there, fully formed in his Nike trainers but oh dear, he could see right through them to a pile of fag-ends on the floor. Just then, a brush wielded by Rita swept through his trainers and pushed the fag-ends into a dustpan.

Dude jumped back. 'I'm ... I'm see-through ... like you ...'

'And that's a fact,' said Grey. 'C'mon, I'll show you more.'

Rita and Doreen were busy clearing up and singing again. 'Who cleans the bogs out? Woof, woof, woof.' Both were still oblivious to the fact they had company, so the boys made their way to Dude's old dressing-room.

'Take a look,' said Grey, gliding through the door and pointing at the floor to ceiling mirror.

Dude went over and gasped. Someone very like himself looked back. Same face, same body, same hair. He wasn't quite as grey as Grey but he was equally transparent.

'I'm still in the same clothes!'

'Yeah. Whatever you die in, you stay in.'

'I thought I'd get a white sheet or something,' he said, then burst out laughing.

'What's so funny?' asked Grey.

'Tara. Always said she could see right through me.'

'How come?'

'Like when I was telling a porkie or something. Don't even bother, she'd say, I can see right through you.'

'Oh I get it. Hey, you're going to be OK,' laughed back Grey. 'It's such a drag sometimes I can tell you. Some people come over all morbid when it happens to them and they start moaning away, 'Oh ... I'm *sooooo saaa*-ad because I'm *traaaan*sparent.' Got no time for that myself. I've moved on. New chapter. You've got to make the best of it. Me. I'm Grey and proud of it. In fact I have a theme song, wanna hear it?'

Dude nodded.

Grey burst into his anthem. 'Sing if you're glad to be Grey ...'

Dude creased up. He was beginning to like his new pal. 'I've got a song as well then,' he laughed as he checked out his new look in the mirror again.

'Hit me,' said Grey.

'I ain't got no ... body ...' sang Dude.

Grey laughed so hard, he blasted himself flat on his back and lay there kicking his legs in an attempt to regain his balance. 'You're the man, Dude. I can tell already, you're going to be one cool ghoul.'

Three

'Now I expect you've got some questions,' said Grey, adopting his official tone as novice ghost's guide.

'Only a quillion,' said Dude. 'Will I ever see Tara again? Or my mum and dad? Or my kid brother Liam? In fact, where will I live now?' What happens next? Do we need to sleep? But most important right now, how do we *eat*? I'm starving.'

'Whoa, slow down, bro',' said Grey. 'We've got loads of time. Hector sent me to show you the ropes so don't worry. You've got a lot to learn but that's why I'm here.'

But Dude wasn't really listening. A delicious smell had hit his nostrils and it was calling out to him. 'Hungry ...' he said.

Grey lifted his nose into the air and sniffed. 'Ah yes. Hot dog stand I do believe. Follow me.'

Dude looked around but couldn't see anything, so with a shrug he followed Grey's fat, floaty form through the car park and out into the street. And there it was, a hot dog stand a hundred metres or so away, outside the underground station.

We're just in time thought Dude, when he saw that the hot dog man was busy packing up for the night.

'Hot dog, mustard and double onions,' said Dude, eagerly eyeing the tray of fat sausages nestling on a bed of golden onions. But the man just picked up the tray and dumped the lot into a black bin-bag.

'Uh? Oh, I forgot. He can't see me can he?'

'You're catching on,' said Grey.

Dude's eye fell on a last hot dog crammed with onions and mustard lying in a paper napkin on the stand. *This one's got my name on it,* he thought, as he reached for it, but his hand went right through it.

'So how do I pick things up?' he asked. 'I tried before with a sandwich, but no joy.'

'Ah. Classic case of hollow hand,' said Grey. 'Here begins lesson one in how to survive the after life. You've got to use your will. You know, like in a dream, sometimes you think something and it just happens.'

'Oh, like visualising? My last girlfriend was into all that. Self help and stuff. Helped herself to most of my CD collection, if I remember rightly.'

'You got to be serious Dude. You have to learn. Use your will.'

'So what should I will?' asked Dude. 'That the hot dog floats off the stand, loops the loop and flies into my mouth?'

Grey shook his head. 'Nah. You will your hand to pick it up. Visualise your hand as a real hand, so open your fingers and go for it.'

Dude nodded but he looked confused. Grey sighed then floated up to the hotdog stand roof where he adopted a professional stance and launched into a mini-lecture.

'Ahem. I'd better explain. See, us ghosts, we're not matter any more. The hot dog is. The hot dog is energy formed as matter. Us, that's you and me pal, we're energy vibrating outside normal human perception. We're in a purer form, like refined energy, which is why we can float through things and people can walk through us. Let me give you an example ...'

'This gonna take long?' asked Dude. 'I'm dying of

hunger here.'

'Oh, he's dying of hunger. That's a good one – but it doesn't really matter anymore,' chortled Grey. 'Geddit? Matter? Doesn't matter? Oh, never mind. You have to concentrate, Dude. Now,' Grey pointed at his own chubby hand, 'watch this, I will the spectral energy flowing through my form to concentrate in my hand.'

Dude looked more confused than ever.

Grey sighed and tried again. 'The atoms that make up matter all hang together and that's what makes things seems solid. Imagine a load of octopuses all linking hands and legs. Loads of them.'

Dude shook his head. 'Atoms, octopus ... what are you on about?'

'OK,' continued Grey launching himself off the roof and floating down towards Dude, 'It sometimes helps to think of it like glue coating your ethereal essence and sticking it all together to make it solid.'

'OK, no problemo,' said Dude. 'All I've got to do is get glue on my essence and ... bung it down my arm into my hand ... imagine I'm an octopus ... Are you *crazy*? I'm hungry and all I get is a crash course in paranormal physics. I didn't get physics in normal life and I certainly don't get your mumbo-jumbo now that I'm dead.'

'Er, we're supposed to call it 'beyond life'...' said Grey, with a weak smile. 'Gloria prefers us to say that.'

'And who's Gloria?'

'Pain in the butt recent arrival. Passed away six months ago. Used to be a social worker.'

'Well, Gloria can take a running jump. All I need is a politically correct ghost.'

'I know,' sighed Grey. 'So enough of her. Come on, that's one yummy looking hot dog, go for it.'

Dude concentrated and tried to will his hand to be heavy. He thought of glue, focused his mind and reached out for the hot dog. No luck, as again, his hand went straight through it.

Oblivious to the drama unfolding before him, the hot dog man muttered to himself about business and continued clearing up his stand. Dude tried again. This time, he screwed up his eyes and really focused but failed to make contact. The mouthwatering aroma of hot sausage, onion and mustard seemed to fill his entire body. He longed to take a bite and made another futile snatch.

'Close but not quite there yet,' said Grey. 'Slow down. Concentrate. Feel that your fingers have weight, form, strength. All those octopuses' atoms hanging together.'

Once more, Dude gathered up his energy and sent it flowing down his hand and it was true, it was beginning to feel heavier. He redoubled his efforts and imagined a bunch of octopuses linking arms and legs, a wave of them flowing down his arm into his hand.

'I think … I think … something's happening … yes, I can feel it working,' he said, in disbelief.

Next thing, the hot dog was in his hand. He raised it to his mouth and shoved it in. Kerflop, the hot dog fell right through him and landed on the pavement.

The hot dog man looked up from his cleaning and stared at the hot dog. 'What the …?' he muttered and dashed round to the front of the stall. 'That was my supper you minging stupid cat,' he yelled as he searched behind a dustbin. 'I'll string you up if I catch you,' he called into thin air then turned back and looked straight at Dude who froze to the spot.

'Hey, chill, he can't see us,' reminded Grey. 'Now, where were we?'

Dude looked down at the splattered hot dog. 'I've heard of food going straight through you but this is ridiculous.'

Grey guffawed. 'Nah. You're doing well, honest. I was just having a bit of fun. You ain't got the innards anymore nor any outards. See, the good news is, you got the hang of holding a material object. That's great, it takes some novices weeks to learn. But the bad news is, you're never going to eat again.'

Dude's face dropped. 'What do you mean *never*?'

'Never ever.'

'Oh *noooo* … no more pepperoni pizza with extra cheese, no more double cheeseburgers or chocolate-shakes, no more Christmas dinner … no more …'

'No more nothing. But it's not that bad,' said Grey. 'You'll get used to it. See, you don't *need* to eat anymore. It's much more convenient and think of the time you'll save on washing up.'

'OK. So why am I hungry? How do we feed? Oh, don't tell me, we have to suck necks like vampires. Ohmigod, I'm a vampire,' he looked around anxiously. 'I'm gonna get staked like in Buffy.'

'No way. Nothing like that. Wake up and smell the onions, kiddo. Haven't you noticed anything about your sense of smell since you passed on?'

Dude shook his head. 'Not really. I don't … hey, yes, that disinfectant back there in the stadium …'

'Exactly,' said Grey. 'That's how ghosts feed. Through their sense of smell.'

'On *disinfectant*? Eeeww.'

'I haven't finished,' said Grey. 'Smell. When you're first born, it's the most powerful sense you have then it fades. Did you know that?'

Dude shook his head again.

'See, when a baby comes into the world, it's brand new and still sniffing, using its most potent sense, that's how it recognises it's mother. Then the ability fades as the other senses become sharper. When you pass on, it comes streaming back. Like,' Grey inhaled deeply, 'mmmm, take a proper hit of those onions.'

Dude bent over the vat of onions and took a long deep sniff. The sensation of onion flooded through his body like warm liquid, a hit of pure pungent sensation.

'Not bad, eh,' said Grey. 'Another cool of being a ghoul. See, smells are vibrations, each with a different frequency. All we have to do is breathe them in. We don't have the messy stuff of chewing, digesting and having to go to the loo and stuff anymore. It's pure. We sniff. That's it.'

Dude was busy with his nose in the hot dog. Four separate smells, the light, yeasty scent of the bread, then a spicy, heavier whiff of sausage, perfect, yum, then the heady aroma of onions followed by the peppery smell of mustard. He had to admit he was enjoying the sensations.

He lifted his head. 'Wow. What a blast. And amazing, I don't feel hungry anymore. I feel satisfied. Full. But light. So no indigestion, no tummy-ache …?'

'Nope. None of that heavy feeling after a meal.'

'So, er, how come you're, um …?'

'How come I'm fat?' asked Grey, smiling.

Dude nodded.

'I was always this way. You don't lose weight when you're dead, I mean beyond life. You have the same form you had when you had a body.'

'So what happened to you? How long ago did you d … d … become um … beyond life?'

'Oh, relax, no one takes much notice of Gloria. How long ago did I die? Five years. Drowned in a duck-pond. But I can tell you, I've been having the time of my after life since. 'Course I was a bit disorientated for a while, everyone is. Then when I got the hang of it, I realised how brilliant it was going to be. I *love* being a ghost.' He burst into his anthem again. 'Sing if you're glad to be Grey.'

Now that Dude's appetite was satisfied, his questions came back thick and fast. 'So what next? What happens now? What do we do with our lives ... I mean deaths ...? We just hang about sniffing stuff or what?'

Grey shook his head. 'Nah. I'll take you to meet the others. One of them in particular has been dying to meet you.'

'Is that possible?' teased Dude.

Grey burst out laughing. 'Boy, you kill me ...' he teased back.

'So where are we going?' asked Dude, as Grey strode away from the stand.

'Your new home,' said Grey. 'Oh, you're going to love it there. All very cosy. There's three of us there. Me, Bella and Bogus.'

'Why can't I go back to my old home?'

'You can if you want but you've got a lot to learn first. In fact a heckofa lot. Starting with, do you *have* to float like that?'

'I kind of like it,' said Dude, floating two feet off the pavement then back again. 'Besides I was worried I might slide through the ground and end up somewhere really weird like the centre of the earth stuck in some red hot magma.'

'Nah, don't worry. You'll get the hang of it soon. It's like when we walk, you can go forward, you can go backwards and sideways. Right? You control when to go and when to stop?'

'Yeah. 'Course.'

'It's the same when you're a ghost only you get additional movements. You can go up, you can go down. It can feel a bit out of control at first, like learning to walk when you're a toddler, but you'll get there. Just takes a bit of practise, so don't worry, it's just like pressing an accelerator or a brake in a car, only it's internal.'

'OK, cool,' said Dude, shooting up a few feet then coming down to settle on the pavement.

Grey floated forward so that he was in line with him. 'OK, let's go together. Ready?' he asked. 'OK. And a ... one two three, one two three ... and forward, up, back and down. Forward, up, back and down.'

Dude fell in alongside him, forward, up, back and down, not missing a step. 'Whoa, this is like doing ballroom dancing,' he laughed, as he added a few hip swivels.

A moment later, they passed a house with all the windows open, and the music to 'Saturday Night Fever' was blasting out.'

Grey chuckled. 'You thinking what I'm thinking?'

Dude nodded and they turned to face each other. They tapped their feet for a few beats until they'd got the rhythm then went into a disco dance routine, only three foot up in the air. When the track changed, Dude collapsed on the pavement laughing. 'OK. Yeah. Got it. Start, stop, start, stop. Up, down, turn around. Boogie-woogie, easy peasy.' He floated up five feet in the air this time and made his body go horizontal. 'OK, Grey, do the fish.' Dude mimicked doing the breast stroke and then the crawl. 'Yeah. It's just like swimming only in the air instead of

29

water. Yeah, feels good,' he said as he made himself go vertical again. 'I get it.'

'Good,' said Grey as they resumed their normal walking pace. 'And it answers the age old mystery. Why ghosts can float through walls but don't sink through the floor. They simply put the old brake on.'

'Yeah,' said Dude. 'I did used to wonder when I watched ghost films.'

'Well, there you go. Mystery over. Still, there are others I didn't get when I was alive. Like where do all the lost socks go? Why can't you get decaffeinated coffee tables? How does the man who drives the snow-plough get to work in the morning?'

'Oh, I can answer that one,' said Dude. 'My old man drove a snow-plough. They watch the weather forecast before they go home then if it looks like snow, they sleep at work ready for the morning.'

'Really? That's brilliant, you'll have to tell Bogus. He spends his days trying to fathom mysteries.'

'Who is this Bogus?'

'One of the gang. Spends all his time on the computer researching what's going on. Spends his life on it, his life ... oh, that's another good one,' said Grey emitting a laugh that sent him chuckling off round the corner like a small, plump tornado.

'Hey, wait for me,' shouted Dude. One thing he definitely didn't want was to get lost so soon into his afterlife.

Rounding the corner, Dude spotted Grey sitting on top of a traffic light, still chortling to himself.

'Now, where were we?' he said as he floated down to Dude.

'Bogus,' said Dude. 'You were telling me about Bogus.'

'Oh, yeah. He's cool. Passed on last summer and still

hasn't accepted it. He says he can't be dead, as he's still here. That's why he's always on the computer researching all he can about us. He scans himself in then surfs the Net.'

'Scans himself in? Nah, go on,' said Dude.

'For real. Says it's something about codes ... once your code is in, you can go anywhere.'

'You're losing me again, man,' said Dude.

'Oh, Bogus'll explain. He's amazing. Quick as a flash, he's through the scanner and away. Sometimes he's gone for hours. Not my scene really as it can be dangerous. Been a bit of trouble lately because of a live kid who's sussed that there are ghosts on the Net. Not a ghost-friendly kind of boy, if you get my meaning. Anyway, I leave all that to Bogus. He's been glued to the computer for weeks now, keeping a watch-out for the boy so it's gonna be OK, not anything for the rest of us to worry about at present. Leave computers to Bogus. I don't really understand any of it.' Grey looked thoughtful for a moment and parked his plump rear on the pavement.

Dude settled next to him. 'He has a point though, this Bogus. I mean I am still here ... sort of. So are you.'

'Yeah, 'course. You only left your body behind. But the being that lived inside it, the vital Dude essence, if you like, that's here.'

Dude nodded in half-agreement.

'I'll put it another way,' said Grey. 'Our bodies are like a top-layer or a set of clothes. We put them on. We look through the eyes, listen through the ears, taste through the mouth, feel through the skin, but the real us, the real being that *does* the feeling, looks out the eyes, does the listening ...'

'Man, you're doing the gobbledegook thing again,' said Dude. 'But I have to say it was weird looking at myself

31

back there, when they were taking me to the ambulance. Like I was an empty shell.'

'Exactly,' said Grey.

'So does everyone become a ghost?'

'I dunno,' shrugged Grey. 'Don't think so. I think some people go straight through.'

'Straight through where?'

'Search me. That's what Bogus is trying to find out. He reckons that those of us on this level, us ghosts, are here for a reason. Unfinished business or some task we have to perform. But none of us knows a whole lot more than when we had bodies.'

Dude looked thoughtful. 'We don't know a lot do we? I mean I never really thought about it before, but us humans are a pretty ignorant lot, aren't we? You know, when it comes to what it's all really about? Life and death and stuff.'

'Yeah,' said Grey. 'Being a ghost makes you think. Before you just take it for granted. You eat, you sleep, you go to school but where we all came from, where we're all going, nobody really gives you the facts. You don't get a manual when you come in and you don't get one when you go out. But hey, you've got me to show you round.'

'Yeah,' said Dude unconvinced.

'Best get on then,' said Grey standing up.

As they made their way down the street, they passed the usual late night pedestrians. A few drunks, kids hanging out, executives hurrying home from work. But they weren't the only ones out and about. Now, Dude could see the others. Ghosts. Loads of them – different ages, *from* different ages, different races, strolling along, window-shopping, mooching about and chatting to each other as they met up.

'I see dead people,' Dude whispered in a frightened voice.

'D'oh ye*ah* ... 'course,' said Grey. 'There's a whole world of us.'

'And those ones,' said Dude pointing at a little girl dressed in Victorian clothes, 'are they in fancy dress or are they like seriously old?'

'Oh, old. Some ghosts have been around for ages.'

'Literally, by the look of it,' said Dude as a Roman soldier walked past and high fived Grey. 'So how come some go up to another level and some stay down here?'

'I told you, that's what Bogus is trying to fathom. Not my area.'

'Wow,' said Dude. 'Imagine if all the people that ever lived were ghosts, there'd be ... like a crisis, overcrowding, millions and millions of ghosts ...'

'Yeah, well luckily some people go straight on, up to the next level. And then dudes like us hang around on this level and go up later.'

'When do you know? I mean, I've just arrived on this level and it's all a bit much, but going up to even *another* level, whoa ... Don't think I'm ready.'

'Exactly,' said Grey. 'There's a lot to learn here. As I said, just because you're a ghost doesn't mean you get all the answers. Like in life. Who knows?'

Dude was beginning to feel depressed. He'd never realised that he was so ignorant before and wished he'd asked more questions when he was alive.

'I was in the cemetery the other day,' said Grey. 'Someone had painted graffiti on one of the gravestones. It had a poem engraved on it, "Stop stranger there as you go by, as you are now, so once was I. As I am now, so you shall be, so be prepared to follow me." Someone had written beside it in white paint, "To follow you I'd be content, if only I knew which way you went."'

'Cool,' said Dude. 'Yeah, you don't know in life what's going to happen. No one talks about it hardly, so yeah, I guess, why should you know all the answers now?'

'Right,' said Grey. 'So chill, you've enough to take in for the moment. One step at a time. I'm sure when we're ready, we'll find out. I reckon it's like at school. People do GCSEs, then A levels, then they go on and do degrees. You never stop learning.' Suddenly, he stopped outside a house and peered in. 'Hey, get a load of this.'

Dude joined him at the window, looked in, then burst out laughing. Inside, an elderly couple were slumped on a sofa watching the telly. They looked a right miserable pair. Like zombies sipping mugs of tea. Behind the sofa however, was a crowd of ghosts laughing, talking, singing, dancing and having a great old time. Locked into an episode of some soap on the telly, Mr and Mrs Zomboid were completely oblivious to them.

These ghosts have really got the floating up, back and sideways routine thought Dude, as he watched one ghost spin up to the lightshade, back flip down into a headstand, then spin around on his head. *Break dancing à la ghostie style*, thought Dude. *It's hip hop heaven.*

'Jade the Shade,' said Grey, as a black girl ghost spotted Grey at the window and gave him a wave. 'It's her death day.'

'Uh?'

'Like a birthday, but here we celebrate the day you passed over.'

'Shall we go in?' asked Dude. He liked a party and this one looked like it was rocking.

Grey looked tempted, then hesitated. 'Nah. Best get

you back. We're late as it is.'

He set off again with Dude behind him and came to a stop outside a red brick house at the end of a terrace. 'And here we are. Home sweet home.

Four

Dude felt apprehensive as he slid through the door after Grey. He remembered what Grey had told him back at the stadium – that in the after life, there are good and bad ghosts just as there are good and bad people. *Maybe bad ghosts live here,* Dude thought. *It's probably going to be like an old castle inside, cold with dark dungeons and eerie laughter coming from unseen rooms. They're bound to be really creepy and spend their nights watching each other through walls, then jumping through just for a laugh. Or walking about with their heads under their arms, putting their eyeballs in jamjars or ... or taking their legs off and hitting each other with the soggy end.* A shiver went down Dude's spine as his imagination went into overdrive.

His fears seemed justified. The house was dark, save for the light of a mass of candles. They lined the hall and the stairs casting giant animal shadows on the walls. *Sinister,* thought Dude.

'So what do you think of the old homestead?' asked Grey, as he led Dude from the hall into a sitting-room complete with large, squashy sofas and a telly.

'Weird,' said Dude, as he took in the landscape painting on the wall, the table lamps, the coffee table with magazines on it, 'Real weird.' It *was* weird. The house was normal. Mega normal. Nothing like he expected.

'We've got all the mod cons,' said Grey. 'Kitchen out the back. Bedrooms on the upper floors ...'

Dude was still looking worried.

'Ah, the candles?' asked Grey. 'That'll be Bella. She's been getting ready for you. Probably trying to create a romantic atmosphere. Yuk.'

Someone coughed behind them and when Dude turned his jaw fell open in shock. It was a girl. No, a babe, standing in the doorway. A babe ghost in Goth clothes with Disney princess eyes and a luscious mouth like a flower.

'Dude, this is Bella Ghostie. Bella this is Dude,' said Grey.

Bella stepped forward and smiled shyly, and for a second, Dude could have sworn her silvery colour turned rose.

'I know who he is dorkbrain,' she said. 'Hi Dude. I'm *so* glad you can see me at last.'

'Er, yeah. Likewise,' gulped Dude, thinking to himself that he'd seen her before somewhere.

'You look kind of familiar,' he smiled at her. 'Have we met before, maybe at one of my gigs?'

'Could be,' she grinned and pulled on a woolly hat.

'You're her … the woolly clad girl!' he said.

'Bella's got a hang up about being invisible,' explained Grey. 'She could go to your gigs like any normal ghost but no, she has to be one of the crowd. Loves a bit of mosh pit mania, don't you?'

Bella nodded. 'You'll be able to do it one day when you've practised a bit. It's takes a bit of time to get ready but it's one way of getting people to talk to you…'

'Whoa, slow down, Bella,' said Grey, 'being visible to live people is way too advanced for Dude at the moment. So butt out, I'm his guide, not you. And he's new to all this, so I'm doing it one step at a time with him. Now. Where was I? Oh, yes, talking to people. See, you can talk to people but they can only hear you if they will it. Can be tricky, as why should they will to hear you if they don't know you're there?'

'And if you touch them or something, they get spooked and act all freaked out, ohmigod, *ohmigod*, there's a *ghost*, gets *sooo* tedious. So if you put some clothes on, they see a recognisable shape and no problemo, there's no hysterics.'

'I *said* butt out, Bella,' warned Grey. 'Don't want to confuse him on his first day.'

'But what about your face? And your eyes?' asked Dude, 'your hands?'

'First you have to will your outer layer to be solid. You have taught him that already haven't you, Grey?'

'Yeah, 'course, lesson numero one wasn't it, Dude?'

Dude nodded.

'OK,' said Bella. 'Then you will your form to be magnetic.'

'Yeah, right,' frowned Dude. 'Magnetic.'

'It's easy,' said Bella. 'All you do is line up the electron orbits in the air atoms around where you've willed your form to be ...'

'*Whaddit*? Electrons, orbits ... Er, is this some kind of new ghost language?' asked Dude feeling like his brain was about to blow a fuse. He didn't get it at all.

'No, honest, it's easy,' said Bella. 'You make sure all the electrons are turning in the same direction because that's what makes them magnetic. With me so far?'

Dude shook his head. 'You lost me back on an orbit somewhere.'

Bella smiled. 'I guess it can be a bit tricky in the beginning as you can get all sorts of stuff sticking to you. Like Grey, he's hopeless at it. He goes overboard on the magnetic bit don't you?'

'No. I can do it,' said Grey, and screwed his eyes up in concentration. A sudden commotion in the hallway diverted Dude's attention. His mouth opened in surprise as he saw a frying-pan come flying out of the kitchen at the back, down the corridor and into the sitting-room.

'*Duck*, Dude,' cried Bella as the pan zoomed in and settled itself on Grey's head. Bella shrieked with laughter. 'See what I mean?' she asked. 'He's got the basic concept but not refined it. *Anything* that's metal is attracted to him. Er ... overload on the magnetic force Grey. Tone it down a bit.'

Grey looked highly embarrassed and gave Dude a lopsided grin.

'Hmm,' laughed Dude as he took in the vision of Grey with a pan on his head. 'Interesting look. I suppose, as expressions go, you could call it deadpan.'

Bella laughed again but Grey looked annoyed with her for making fun of him.

'I'll get the hang of it one day,' he said, taking the pan off his head. 'I just need to work on it a while.'

'Yeah, right. So, anyway,' continued Bella. 'When you've got your electron orbits balanced just right, not like Grey, you get the fake tan out. Not just any old fake tan though, I had to try loads until I found the right one, one with *metallic* ingredients. Sunkiss by Ghoulain. It works because it's got nickel-copper praesodymium alloy in it. A good once over with the old spray and it sticks to you. Contact lenses on the eyes, gloves on the hands and away you go.'

'Sounds *way* too complicated,' said Dude as he looked closely at her. Her enormous eyes were brown, whereas at the gig they'd been luminous green. Then another thought struck him.

'You were in the crowd weren't you? At the stadium? You and a bunch of others. I remember now, I was surfing the crowd and you reached out for me but I went crashing through … and …' Dude reran the events in his mind and suddenly the penny dropped. 'Hey, you *killed* me!'

'Did not,' pouted Bella. 'It was your time anyway. Bogus got an e-mail from Hector. Meet Dude Harris Friday night. Another kid would have dropped you, I was trying to make it easier …'

All further discussion was interrupted by a loud guffaw from upstairs.

'Hey, guys,' called a voice from up the stairs. 'You've *got* to see this.'

Dude followed Grey and Bella into the hall. He watched with amazement as Bella and Grey slid *up* the banister to the first floor. *Yeah, why not* he thought, *when in ghost land, do as the ghosts do*, and he settled himself on the banister and zoomed up after them. They led him into a bedroom that resembled a library. The shelves that lined every wall were heavy with books – the bed, the floor, every surface was covered with papers and files. In the midst of the mayhem, there was a small boy with white hair and owl-like spectacles, bent over a computer.

He looked Dude up and down. 'Oh, the new boy,' he said, taking off his glasses to give them a polish. 'Member of a boy band, I believe.'

Bella pushed Dude forward. 'Bogus, Dude,' she said. 'Dude, Bogus. Bogus is a computer genius and the brains in our ghostie community.'

Bogus nodded briefly towards Dude, then turned back to his screen. 'E-mail from Gloria,' he said, before Dude could ask what his problem with boy bands was.

Grey sighed wearily. 'What does she want this time?'

Bogus sniggered and read from his screen in a high, snooty voice. 'A memo to all departments. From now on, all those who have passed on are to be referred to as 'mortally challenged' as the term ghost is seen to be offensive to some parties.'

All the mortally challenged in the room cracked up, even Dude.

'Oh, give me a break,' he said. 'PC in the afterworld. I thought I'd left all that stuff behind me.'

Grey rolled his eyes then grinned at Dude. 'E-mail her back and say that we object. Say it is our right to be known as what we want, in fact, from now on, we wish to be known as the Dead Dudes.'

'Yeah,' cried Bella. 'The Dead Dudes and I'll be a dudette.'

'Yeah, cool,' said Dude. 'But I get Gloria. My dad had one of those PC thingies. When he'd had one too many, he'd say, "I'm not drunk, I'm spiritually disorientated."' *Come to think of it, I feel a bit spiritually disorientated myself*, he thought. *Why am I still here? Why am I a ghost?*

'So, do you know what this ghost thing is all about?' asked Dude.

'I'm learning,' said Bogus, consulting his notes. 'As far as I can make out there are many levels of existence. Being human is one of them, ghosts another. There's lots more, animal, vegetable, insect, and so on. Why and what for I don't know yet. It's a biggie. What I have found out is that ghosts stay here either because they're in shock and need some time to adjust, or they have a message for someone still alive or, simply, they're not ready for the next level yet.'

Dude's eyelids were growing heavy. So much had happened so fast. He felt wearier than he'd ever felt and longed to close his eyes and forget everything, levels, being mortally challenged, willing his hands to be octopuses with glue stuck all over them, the lot. *Maybe it will be all right here after all,* he thought, as sleep beckoned him. *The house wasn't so spooky and the other ghosts seemed, well, OK ... as far as ghosts went.*

'Oh, look at you, Dude,' said Bella. 'You must be exhausted, first day and everything. You need a good night's sleep and it will all seem a whole lot better in the morning.'

'So we *do* sleep?'

'D'oh, *yeah*,' said Bogus.

'Well I did wonder ...' said Dude. 'Don't forget I'm new to all this.'

'Sleep. Dreams. That's another of the levels I'm researching,' said Bogus. 'Every night humans and ghosts lay down and blast off to all kinds of places. Then, come the morning and here we all are again. It's fascinating.' He looked Dude up and down again. 'Probably over your head though.'

Ah, that's it thought Dude. *He thinks I'm thick.* But he hadn't the energy to get into an argument over the fact that some members of boy bands did actually have brains. 'Sleep, dreams, sounds good to me ...' he yawned.

'I'll show you where you are, then fix you a hot chocolate to sniff,' said Bella.

She ushered Dude up to a tidy, white room on the second floor. Like the rest of the house, it was completely normal. No eyeballs in jam jars, not a disembodied hand anywhere in sight.

I think I'll be comfortable here, thought Dude, as he took in the bed with the brightly coloured patchwork quilt, the big old chest of drawers, and comfy chair by the fireplace. Someone had even put a Dirty Laundry poster up on the wall.

'To make you feel at home,' said Bella, indicating the poster, then she disappeared only to reappear minutes later with a steaming mug of chocolate.

Dude inhaled deeply. A thick, creamy vapour filled his nostrils, reaching from the top of his head to the tips of his fingers. 'Wow! Amazing.' He grinned at Bella.

'Thanks,' she said. 'Now tuck yourself up and I'll see you in the morning. I'm only next door if you need anything.'

Dude lay down on the bed and felt himself start to float through it. He was heading for the floor, through the floorboards, and his head went through the ceiling of the first floor. *Whoops,* he thought as he pulled himself back up. *I'm a lightshade. Forgot, I have to will myself to stop going down or up. Got to put the brake on or else I'll end up right back on the ground floor.* He brought himself back up through the floor and onto the bed, got himself comfy and then mentally put on his brake ability. *Cool,* he thought, *I'm getting the hang of this, it's as easy as going forwards and backwards. Just got to remember.* Dude put his head down on the pillow. It smelt of lavender. Clean, sweet, safe. Within seconds, he was fast asleep.

Five

Dude opened his eyes to find himself floating two feet above his bed. *Kaboola*, he thought, *that was some dream ... ghosts, death and mucho weirdosity, then home safe in my room, playing my CD's, but ... if I'm floating, I must still be dreaming!* He closed his eyes and tried to wake up, but when he opened his eyes again, he was aware of air between him and the bed. He was still floating, only this time a little higher. He looked at his hand and he could see through it to the bed sheets below. Then he looked at the rest of his body. Yes, that was transparent too. *What's going on?* he asked himself, as he desperately tried to ignore the panic surging through him.

He looked around the room but nothing seemed familiar, then the events of the night at the stadium came flooding back. *Oh no*, he thought, *that was no dream. This is really happening*.

He glided across the room and out of the door into the corridor.

'Hey, Dude,' said Grey, coming out of a room opposite. 'You've been out for days. Sleep well?'

'Yeah. *No*,' said Dude. 'Aren't I still asleep and you're in my dream?'

Grey nodded knowingly. 'Had one of those "I'm still alive dreams" did you? Happens a lot in the beginning.'

'Er, yes and no, more like ... oh I don't know,' said Dude, as he went to sit at the top of the stairs and began to float through them, until he remembered he had to put his brake on so that he stayed sitting on the top step. 'Man, I'm confused. I feel like I'm in a place between nowhere and nothing.'

Grey sat next to him. 'Come downstairs. We've got a lot to get through today. And hey, you've got to meet Mrs Riley.'

Dude looked at him quizzically. 'Another ghost?'

'Nah. Bogus's gran. She lets us all stay here. She's really cool, she looks after us and gets Bogus all the stuff he needs for his computer and that. See, one of the rules of being a ghost is you can't stay anywhere you haven't lived or had some kind of association with. Sensible I guess, otherwise, we'd all be hanging out in Kylie Minogue's bedroom. After Bogus passed on, his parents went to live with his sister in Australia to get away from the sad memories. He didn't want to go with them as they couldn't see him. Luckily his gran could and she invited him to come and live with her as she had this big empty house. She's seen ghosts all her life. Means we don't get bothered and well, it's company for her.'

''Suppose,' said Dude, weakly. 'But where were you before?'

'Bella and I were in a squat. Squats and empty buildings are allowed, but they tend to get overcrowded with ghosts who don't like being at their old homes.'

'Why don't they like being at home?'

'All sorts of reasons. Frustration mainly. Seeing people you know carry on as though you're not there. Gets annoying, believe me. Like, try as I might, when I hung about my old house after my funeral, I couldn't get my mum and dad to hear or see me. Then I met Bella and she'd found this empty squat to live in.'

'Why didn't she stay in the house where she lived when she was alive?' asked Dude.

'Oh, it was demolished years ago. Anyway, the squat wasn't great, not like here, but it was home. We kept it clean and no one bothered us, until some bloke bought it, and after that it was never the same … he never washed and with our heightened sense of smell, you can imagine…. Smelly socks, awful BO, yu*rgh*, his entire body reeked like the inside of a wrestler's jockstrap, the stink was *too* bad.'

'Talking of which,' said Dude, 'Do we need to change and wash and stuff. What happens?'

'Nah. I told you, you're not matter any more so you don't rot or get dirty.'

'Brill,' said Dude. 'Always hated washing … but what happens? Do we age now, or stay the same?'

'Stay the same. What you see is how you'll stay.'

'Forever young,' said Dude.

'Yeah, like Bella.'

'Why? How old's Bella?'

'She was fifteen when she died, but she died over a hundred years ago. But don't tell her I told you that.'

'I won't. Amazing. Over a hundred. So she's like the original Goth. Cool. And the Goth look is worn everywhere so that's why she doesn't look out of place?'

'Yeah,' said Grey, 'she fits in now – but she said she felt strangely dressed in the middle part of the last century.'

'But how come we stay young?'

'Whatever age you died at, you stay at. But why or how, that's Bogus's territory. He's researching all …' Grey stopped mid-sentence and took a deep sniff of the air. Dude got it too. A delicious aroma filled the house.

'Mmmm, bacon,' said Dude.

46

He followed Grey down the stairs and into the kitchen where a tiny old lady with white hair was bending over a frying-pan. He couldn't help noticing that she was wearing a T-shirt with the words 'Ghouls Rule' in the middle of a big red heart. Dude looked at Grey for an explanation.

'Mrs Riley, Dude,' was all he said.

'Hello, sweet pea,' she said, looking at Dude. 'Sorry I wasn't up when you got in last night, but have to get your beauty sleep at my age.'

'You can see me?'

She nodded. 'And what a lovely looking boy you are, too. Just like on your posters. Bella showed me them. She's a big fan of yours.'

The smell of bacon was wafting up Dude's nostrils invitingly. He leant over the pan and inhaled. *Yum*, he thought as the aroma coursed through him.

'Excuse me, young man,' said Mrs Riley. 'Manners please.'

'Sorry,' said Dude, straightening up. 'I'm still a bit new to all this.'

'That's all right, love. Now sit down and I'll get you a plate.'

Dude and Grey sat at the kitchen table, and as Dude looked around, he felt sad.

'Remind you of home, does it?' said Mrs Riley, gently.

Dude nodded. 'I want to go and see how my folks are doing.'

''Course you do, love,' said Gran. 'But don't get your expectations up. They might not know you're there. Now get stuck into this,' she said, holding a cup of coffee under his nose. 'You need a good sniff to see you through the day.'

Dude didn't answer. He was still thinking about his family. Mrs Riley gave Grey a look and Grey nodded.

'OK Dude,' he said, standing up, then cupping his hands to his mouth he bellowed, 'Road trip!'

Dude and Grey stood on the pavement opposite Dude's old home as a black hearse covered in flowers pulled up outside. The coffin was covered in flowers spelling out DUDE, A LOVING SON on the side.

'Oh, very tasteful,' said Grey, clearly looking impressed.

'Yeah, but this is weird,' said Dude, pointing at the coffin. 'I'm in there and I'm out here.'

'Don't think of it like that,' said Grey. 'Think of it like you just shed the clothes you were wearing a few days ago and that's what's in the coffin.'

Grey's words offered no comfort.

'Let's go in and see how they're getting on,' he said.

Inside, Pete and Mo Harris were dressed in their best clothes. Pete in his blue suit and Mo in black. Both of them were paler than pale. *White as ghosts,* Dude thought to himself.

'You all right, love?' asked Pete Harris.

'Didn't sleep very well,' answered Mo, tears welling up in her eyes. 'I ... I can't believe he's not coming back.'

Pete sat at the kitchen table next to her as she dabbed her eyes with an already damp handkerchief. He put his hand over hers and they sat in silence, locked in their grief over losing their son.

Dude's eyes filled with tears at seeing his parents so distraught. 'Hey Mum, Dad, it's OK, I'm here. I'm OK,' he said.

Grey touched his arm. 'They can't hear you,' he said.

'Liam,' Mo called up the stairs. 'The car's here.'

A sudden commotion on the stairs announced the arrival of the Harris's youngest son. He looked white as well and his eyes were bloodshot from crying. Dude felt a lump in his throat at seeing him so upset. He loved his little brother dearly.

'All right, kid?' asked Pete.

Liam nodded. 'Just been in his bedroom ... but it's true, isn't it? Our Dude really has gone.'

'No, *NO*, I'm here, *right* in front of you,' said Dude, who desperately wanted to reassure them and find a way to make them feel better.

Liam sat at the table with them. 'I went to check in his room because last night, I dreamt he was here, playing his CDs and mucking about as usual. It was so real.'

'I wish,' said Mo.

'Well, we'd best get sorted,' said Pete, standing up. 'Get to the funeral ...'

The small family group trooped out to the car at the front and got in.

'We should go with them,' said Grey. 'Otherwise we'll have to get the bus.'

'Can't we just whizz there? At the stadium, I was going up and down real fast.'

Grey shook his head. 'Happens in the beginning when your up, down ability first kicks in, but after that you'll find you can only go up a short distance at first, so it's either glide or public transport. Some of the older ghosts can teleport but it takes some doing. Can take years to learn. Still, in the meantime the good thing is we don't have to pay for transport any more. 'Course you could hitch a ride in any car that goes past, but it's not always a good idea.

I got in a sproncy Merc once and whoa, before I knew it, I ended up in Bognor.'

'Why didn't you just float out?' asked Dude.

'Yeah, right,' said Grey. 'Want to try that when a car is going sixty miles an hour? I don't think so. That's the problem, you don't always know where cars are going. Like you want a ride to the corner shop, but the car drives right past and then before you know it, you're speeding down a motorway to who knows where. 'Planes, now they're different. You know where they're going. Says on the destination board. In fact, we're all going on holiday one day, when we can agree on where to go.'

'Can I come?'

'What on hols? Yeah. 'Course. It's good for the spirit,' chuckled Grey.

'Where're you going to go?' asked Dude.

''We're thinking about having a week in the Dead Sea in Israel then off to tour Death Valley in the States,' said Grey, as Dude looked out the window.

'Quick, they're going,' he said. 'Don't want to be late for my own funeral.'

'Dead Sea, geddit?' chuckled Grey, as Dude hauled him out the front door. They were just in time to see the funeral limo driving off down the street whilst a crowd of neighbours stood around sniffling into handkerchiefs.

'I don't believe it!' cried Dude. 'What do we do now?"

Grey indicated the bus-stop a short distance away from the house.

Dude shook his head. 'Oh *no*. I don't believe it. Got to get a *bus* to my own bloomin' funeral!'

They raced off down the road to the bus-stop where an old man was waiting with his granddaughter.

The bus came after five minutes and Dude and Grey climbed on. It was more than crowded so Grey settled himself comfortably on a teenaged girl's knee.

'See what I mean? he asked Dude. 'Told you it was good being a ghost.'

Dude couldn't bring himself to sit on anyone's knee no matter how pretty. He stood in the aisle and as the bus lurched forward, his nose pushed up against a tall bloke's armpit.

He reeled back. 'Phorrr! This sense of smell thing has a distinct disadvantage. I think I'm going to pass out.'

'Yeah, you do look kind of green,' said Grey.

As a wave of nausea swept over Dude, he felt he was going to faint. The smells from the bus were overwhelming him. He could tell what everyone had had for dinner last night. The bloke at the back stank of beef curry, a woman in front reeked of garlic, a little girl beside her smelt of cheese and sour milk and a baby, oh no, he'd clearly done an almighty poo in his nappy. Essence of puried vegetables and ... and mashed banana wafted Dude's way. Turning away, Dude's nostrils were assaulted by a new horror coming from a glamorous girl seated at the front. *Phew*, it was her perfume. Yeeurghh, stank of rat do mixed with lemon, vanilla and battery acid.

'Can't take the ... the smells,' said Dude, holding his nose. 'They're coming at me from everywhere ...'

Grey chuckled and floated off the lap he was on. He bent over and started limping up the aisle. 'The smells, the *smells*,' he moaned in Hunchback of Notre Dame fashion.

'I thought you were supposed to be helping me,' said Dude weakly.

Grey stood up straight. 'Sorry. You'll get used to it. I'll give you a pair of nose-plugs when we get home later, just to see you through the early days. Needed them myself in the early days. Hang on, you'll be OK in the future.'

'That's if I make it through today,' groaned Dude.

A few stops later and they were at the church.

'It's the one at the end of the road I think,' said Dude, making his way towards a church on the corner.

'So come on or we'll miss the best bits,' said Grey. 'Don't you want to see who's turned up? Come on, it's a once in a lifetime experience.' A huge guffaw sent him spiralling backwards into the arms of a monumental angel that stood in the cemetery at the front of the church.

'Looks like everyone's inside,' said Dude, looking round. He couldn't help feeling disappointed. 'Where are all my fans? I know fame doesn't last long these days, but this is insulting!'

'Maybe they didn't know that today was the day, or maybe they're inside,' said Grey, heading for the door.

Inside the church, the sweet, woody scent of frankincense hit their nostrils.

'Umm, nice pong,' said Grey, as they made their way up the aisle. 'Clears your chest.'

The service had already started so they hurriedly sat down at the back of the congregation and listened.

'He lived a good life ...' said a man at the front.

Grey gave Dude the thumbs up and Dude nodded back in approval. So far, so good.

'His work for charity was boundless ... his time in Africa ... he'll be sadly missed by his six children.'

Grey looked over at Dude and winked. '*Six*,' he mouthed. 'Respect.'

But Dude was looking confused. He glanced round the church. Not a familiar face in sight. Then the penny dropped.

'It's the *wrong* bloomin' church,' he hissed at Grey.

Six

'You take that way,' said Dude, pointing down a broad avenue with a couple of church steeples visible in the distance. 'I'll work my way back down the High Street.'

Grey nodded and sped off.

'If you see anything, then whistle,' called Dude after him. 'You can whistle can't you?

Grey blew him an ear-piercer. *The answer is clearly yes*, thought Dude, as he raced off in the opposite direction.

'Seen a funeral anywhere?' he breathlessly asked an old lady ghost who passed him on the street.

'Oh, I've seen a lot of funerals in my time, dear,' she said, settling in for a good old natter. 'I love a good send off ...'

'No I mean *today*, near here?'

The lady looked offended that Dude was in such a hurry but she pointed down the road.

'Chapel on the corner of Barker Street there's a big crowd. Lots of kids...'

Dude was off. He whistled to Grey to join him and they sped as fast as they could down the street.

'Over there,' called Dude, as he spotted a crowd of tearful teenagers sitting amongst the graves in a churchyard. Some of them were waving candles, others softly singing the words of Dude's hit single.

'This has to be it,' said Dude, pointing to a teenaged girl wearing a Dirty Laundry T-shirt.

'Hey, good turn out,' said Grey, surveying the crowd.

'Yeah,' said Dude. 'Now let's get inside.'

Every space and pew in the church was packed.

'This is more like it,' whispered Dude, as he led the way up the aisle and sat down next to his mum and Liam. He felt sad watching his mum snuffling into her handkerchief. He longed to put an arm round her and tell her what a great mum she'd been. *It's true* he thought, *it's much harder for those left behind.*

'Hey, Ma,' he said. 'I'm all right and I had a good life, bit short yeah but hey, my last single got to number one. Some people don't get close to that in a lifetime...'

'She can't hear you,' whispered Grey.

'I know that,' said Dude, looking round at the congregation. 'Just thought the intent of what I was saying might get through. Hey, should be a good do, everyone's here.' He felt really chuffed that so many of his mates and family had turned out to see him off, not to mention the hundreds of teenaged fans.

Pete Harris had climbed into the pulpit and Dude fell silent to hear what his dad was saying about him.

'... he was a good lad, generous and big-hearted ...'

Dude smiled approvingly and whispered to Grey. 'I read about this once at school. Tom Sawyer, he went to his own funeral.'

'Yeah,' said Grey, 'but he was still alive. And you don't have to whisper. No one can hear you.'

'Oh, yeah. Keep forgetting.'

'Woof-woof double cor!' said Grey, pointing to a pretty young girl in the second pew back who was crying her heart out.

Dude turned and his eyes softened. 'That's Tara Jacobs. She's, that is *was*, my girlfriend.' She was sitting with her mum and her mate Jenni and she did look good. *Clearly got a new outfit for the send-off, black always suited her,* he thought as he went over and slid in beside her. He instinctively reached for her hand. No reaction. Then he remembered what Grey had told him about visualising his hand to be real, so summoning all his imagination, he willed his hand to have weight. Again he touched Tara's hand.

'*AhwaGGHH,*' she screamed.

'Yeah,' whispered Jenni. 'That's right. Let it all out ...'

'Bu ... but something just touched my hand,' cried Tara. 'It was cold.'

Dude moved away fast and sat back up front with Grey. *Best wait until I can see her alone,* he thought. *Don't want her freaking out in public. Besides, I want to listen to the rest of the service.*

Dude's old school-mate Mark from the band was next up front. He had his guitar with him and delivered a tender acoustic arrangement of the band's greatest hits.

'Nice, good choice, man,' said Dude who was beginning to really enjoy himself. 'What did you have played at yours Grey?'

'Some crapola I'd never heard of. No one expected me to go, least of all me, and it's not the kind of thing you put on your Christmas list is it? And PS Santa, this is my choice of music for my funeral. So I never had a chance to say what I would have liked. There were some gloomy old hymns and the guy doing the service even called me by the wrong name. Graham. As if.'

'Hey, I wonder if I'm to be buried or cremated? *Eww.* Don't fancy either,' said Dude.

'Don't forget you're not in there any more,' said Grey, eyeing the coffin. 'Anyway, the options stink, I mean would you rather rot and get eaten by worms down under, or be burnt and put in a vase?'

'Hhmmm. Tough call, man,' said Dude. 'My gran was cremated and put on the mantelpiece at granddad's house. My mum went over there to tidy up one day and knocked it over. It was gruesome. Ashes all over the carpet. She felt real bad as she had no choice in the end but to hoover Gran up. Just couldn't separate her from the carpet fluff.'

'My ashes were put in the garden,' said Grey. 'Under an apple tree. Really nice, I thought, until Duchess our old cat started using my grave as her lavvie.'

When Mark finished, one of Dude's aunts got up to do a reading, so Dude decided to have a wander and see who else was there and what the sob factor was. Yeah, there was Shawn from the band. He looked pretty freaked, tears in his eyes. *Excellent,* thought Dude. *Loved you too, man. Mrs Jones next door, yeah, she's having a good blub. Must have forgiven me for the time I broke her window playing footie. And there's Mary Beasley. Cow. She's not crying at all, I knew she never really liked me.* He considered giving her a chilly finger up the nose when he heard the voice of his old music-teacher coming from the pulpit.

'Dude's talent was evident from an early age …'

Dude sat back down next to his mum and lapped up all the tributes as a stream of people got up and said what a lovely boy he'd been – talented, kind, bright. How much he'd be missed by friends, family, fans all over the world.

'It's just like This is Your Life,' said Dude. 'You know, off the telly.'

'Yeah,' sobbed Grey who had tears in his eyes. 'Only this is your death. It's all very moving.'

Dude however was enjoying every minute. *My kind of do,* he thought. *I never knew I was such a great guy.*

Soon it was time to take the coffin away and everyone stood as the last piece of music began to play.

'A special request from Dude's granddad,' announced Pete Harris as the opening bars filled the church. Suddenly Dude's eyes filled with tears and he let out an anguished sob.

'Hey, Dude, I told you, it's not the real you in the coffin,' comforted Grey.

'Nah, it's not that,' said Dude as 'Wish Me Luck As You Wave Me Goodbye' blasted out through the loudspeakers. 'It's the music. It's *so* uncool. I would *never* have chosen this. I could die.'

Grey blasted back in his usual manner. 'Oh, get a life,' he chuckled.

The military band piece soon faded and the chords of the Beatles' song 'Hey Jude' filled the air. Everyone sang along only they sang 'Hey Dude' instead of 'Jude.'

'Yeah, nice,' said Dude, nodding his head with approval. 'That's better.'

After that an all time favourite from his dad's old vinyl collection started up. It was Led Zeppelin playing 'Stairway to Heaven'. A lump rose in Dude's throat. He knew exactly why his dad had chosen it as they used to listen to it together before Dude had learnt to play guitar. They used to get the tennis-rackets out, pretend that they were guitars, and play along with the band. As he reminisced, an idea suddenly occurred to Dude and he couldn't resist.

He floated up on top of his coffin where he began to play air guitar along with the soundtrack.

'Party time,' he cried as the snuffling congregation filed

out. Dude was into a crescendo of wild arm air chords when suddenly he heard someone laughing. Dude looked in the direction of the sound.

It was Bella and she floated up to join him.

'Rock on, Dude,' she said.

'I intend to,' he said, continuing his air guitar playing as the coffin was carried out. 'Amazing isn't it? All these people crying over me and here I am.'

As the coffin bearers reached the path outside the chapel, Dude took Bella's hands in his and flung both their arms wide open like Leonardo di Caprio and Kate Winslet in "Titanic". 'I'm king of the world,' he shouted to his fans. 'Rock and roll will *never* die.'

Outside, Dude, Grey, and Bella mingled with the crowd gathered to wish the Harris family well and give their condolences.

'I tell you, I felt something,' Dude heard Tara tell Jenni. 'It was Dude. I'm sure it was him, trying to communicate.'

Dude stood next to her and put his arm round her.

She leapt back. 'There, *here*. I felt it again. I'm positive it's Dude.'

She wheeled round and looked Dude straight in the eyes.

'Tara,' he said but her gaze moved on, scanning the air.

'Dude, Dude is that you?'

One of the teenaged fans was watching her and nudged her friend. 'Total nutter that bird of his. Look at her. She's lost it. Whassup love. Seen a ghost?'

'Shut up,' said Jenni, as she led Tara away. 'Let's go, Tara. Mrs Harris has invited us back to their house. You up to it?'

Tara shook her head. 'No. Too many memories there. Anyway, I've had a better idea. Let's go home and try and contact Dude. I know he's about here somewhere.'

'But how?' asked Jenni.

'Dunno yet,' said Tara. 'But I'll think of something.'

Dude watched as his family got back into the funeral car and the rest of the crowd began to disperse.

'Where to now, Dudester?' asked Grey. 'Back for a bit more ego boosting at the wake?'

Dude watched his parents drive off then looked for Tara. She was getting into a car with her mum and Jenni and ... someone else.

'Nah, not home,' cried Dude. 'Bella's gone with Tara. Quick. Follow those girls.'

Seven

A grey Volvo with Tara in it was pulling away as Dude and Grey reached the road. Bella saw them and gave them a cheeky wave out of the back window.

'Heck, heck, heckity heck,' said Grey. 'She's up to something. She's always been jealous of Tara. Quick, grab the bumper.'

Grey accelerated ahead, launched himself at the car and grabbed onto the back bumper as it moved off into the traffic. Dude wasn't so fast.

'Hold on to my legs,' cried Grey, as the car jolted ahead.

Without thinking, Dude did as he was told and flew forwards. He grabbed on with one hand and off they zoomed down the street.

It wasn't a long journey as Tara only lived a few streets away but with every gear change, Dude slipped further back until in the end, he was clinging onto Grey's ankles.

'You ... OK ... back ... there ...?' wheezed Grey as the exhaust pipe belted smoke out at them.

'Just ... about ...' Dude spluttered, as he held on with all his strength.

Buses, taxis, cars were whizzing by beside them. Shops, churches, the cinema. Dude couldn't help noticing a group of ghosts coming down the steps from the cinema. They stopped, pointed and started laughing. *Yeah, yeah,* he thought, *must look very amusing, a Volvo driving past with two ghosts hanging onto the back, their bodies flying out horizontally behind them.*

'Me and Jenni want to be by ourselves,' said Tara when they arrived back at Tara's house.

''Course love. I understand,' said Mrs Jacobs. 'You go on up to your room and I'll bring you a nice cup of tea in a while.'

Whilst the girls – followed by Bella – trooped upstairs, outside, Grey and Dude tried to untangle themselves from where they'd landed on top of each other in a heap, when the car stopped.

'Remind me not to do that again in a hurry,' gasped Dude.

'Don't do that again in a hurry,' said Grey.

Dude punched him. 'Fat lot of good you are as a guide,' he said. 'First of all you take me on the smelliest bus in the universe, then you almost get us killed on the way over here.' Then he realised what he'd said and grinned sheepishly.

Grey grinned back. 'Then, as your guide, I reckon we ought to get up there double-quick before Bella does something we'll regret.'

Dude followed Grey as he slid through the front door and up the stairs. Once in Tara's bedroom, they surveyed the scene.

It all looked peaceful enough. Tara was rummaging through drawers pulling out everything that she could find that reminded her of Dude. Bella, in the meantime, had seated herself cross-legged on a bean-bag on the floor.

'Hi, boys,' she said. 'Enjoy the ride?'

'What are you up to?' asked Grey.

'Who *me*? Oh, nothing,' she smiled as she watched Tara gather her Dude memorabilia and put it on the floor in the middle of the room. So far, it consisted of a poster of Dirty Laundry's first gig, a framed photo of her and

Dude from last summer, one of his fleeces, and a couple of CDs.

'I wondered where that was,' said Dude, glancing at one of the CDs.

'Now what do we do?' asked Jenni.

'Should be a synch according to my Auntie Betty,' said Tara, rolling her eyes and starting to sway. 'She's a clairvoyant and she said I had psychic gifts. Come from a long line of psychic women in fact.'

'So what do we do?'

'We draw an invisible circle, sit in it and call Dude to contact us.'

'Did Auntie Betty teach you that?' asked Jenni.

'Nah. Seen it on telly. Sabrina I think.'

'Cool.'

'Yeah, just call me Tara the teenage witch.'

The girls drew a circle in the air then sat down inside it.

'Oh, Dudester,' said Tara to the ceiling.

'I'm over here,' said Dude, standing right in front of her.

'If you're there,' continued Tara, 'Please make yourself known.'

Bella stepped into the circle, picked up the photograph frame and with a wicked smile at Dude, she hurled it against the wall.

'*Ohmigod*,' cried Jenni leaping up and heading for the door, 'There's something in here. I never expected it to work.'

'N ...n ...neither did I,' whispered Tara.

'*Bella!*' said Dude, leaping into the circle and grabbing Bella as she began to tear up his poster. 'Cut that out.'

'Dude,' cried Tara. 'Is that you?'

Bella threw the poster aside and picked up Dude's old fleece. 'Why don't you speak to Tara since she's trying so

63

hard to get through?' she taunted, pulling the fleece over her head.

Dude tugged at the sleeve of his fleece. 'Leave off Bella,' he said. 'This isn't funny.'

'Dude? Dude? Is that you?' asked Tara again.

'Yeah Tara, *Tara* ... right here,' said Dude, busily wrestling Bella to get his fleece.

Tara ran to join Jenni at the door. She looked pretty freaked as the empty fleece appeared to contort itself around the room.

'Tara, *Tara*, don't worry, it's *me*, Dude,' said Dude, as Bella once more escaped from his grasp.

Bella laughed. 'Tara, Tara. Hah. Now *she* knows how it feels to be ignored.'

'Pack it in, Bella,' said Grey.

Dude knew he had to act fast, so he willed his hands to glue up and when they felt solid, he went over and took Tara's hand in his. The minute he touched her, she screamed as if she was being murdered.

'Tara,' cried Dude, shaking her. 'It's *me*. It's OK.'

'Oh, that's really comforting.' Bella laughed at Tara who looked as if she was going to faint. 'Why not try that again?'

'Why can't you hear me, Tara?' pleaded Dude.

'She has to will it,' said Grey. 'And with Bella frightening the living daylights out of her, no chance there, pal.'

Behind them, Bella was throwing cushions around and enjoying herself immensely.

'I *said* cut it out, Bella,' cried Grey.

'Yeah, *please*,' begged Dude. 'You're freaking the girls.'

'There's something in the room and I don't think it's Dude,' said Jenni, opening the door. 'I'm getting out of here.'

Tara was out behind her, as quick as a flash, so Dude ran after them.

'Tara, Tara...' he called down the stairs.

'Absolutely brilliant, Bella,' said Grey, starting to put everything back into its place and tidying up. 'Why did you have to go and do that?'

'All is fair in love and war,' giggled Bella. 'I heard her at the gigs calling me a weirdo. Me? As *if.*'

'What's all the commotion?' said Mrs Jacobs from the foot of the stairs.

'We ... we were trying to reach Dude,' sobbed Jenni as she collapsed on the stairs. 'And something else came and started throwing things about.'

'Oh, for heaven's sake!' said Mrs Jacobs as she made her way up the stairs towards the bedroom.

'Mum, *no*,' cried Tara. '*Don't* go in there. It might get you.'

'Nonsense,' said Mrs Jacobs, striding into the bedroom.

By now, Grey was sitting on Bella and holding her hands down so she couldn't start that again.

Mrs Jacobs surveyed the scene. 'Well, everything looks OK to me,' she said, looking at the poster. 'Except this poster is torn a little.'

Tara and Jenni crept back up the stairs where they hovered at the door not daring to go in.

'Honestly, Tara,' said Mrs Jacobs. 'You should know better. Trying to reach Dude indeed. I know it's hard, love, but he's gone. Now you settle down and I don't want to hear any more nonsense. I know it's painful but you have to try to move on.'

'You tell her, missus,' said a muffled voice underneath Grey.

Dude sighed. 'Useless,' he said, as Mrs Jacobs went back down the stairs.

Bella was wriggling underneath Grey's fat form. 'Get off, you big oaf,' she said. 'You're squashing me.'

'Not until you promise to behave,' he said.

'Promise,' said Bella, 'I've made my point.'

Tara and Jenni peeked into the room in amazement. Everything was back in its place.

'I don't want to go back in there,' said Jenni, darting back into the hall.

'Me neither,' said Tara. 'I didn't imagine it, did I?'

Jenni shook her head. 'No. I saw it too. There was something there. Something evil.'

'Evil? *Moi?* Oh get a life, Barbie,' sighed Bella.

'And I felt something,' said Tara. 'Cold … and slimy.'

'Losing your touch, Dudester,' laughed Grey, as Dude looked offended.

'We have to do something,' said Jenni. 'Whatever it was may still be around.'

'Like what?' said Tara.

'You've seen "Ghostbusters" haven't you?' We have to get rid of whatever malignant force is there in the room.'

Dude laughed. 'Oh, for heaven's sake! I see what you mean now Grey … about people always thinking ghosts are scary.'

'Yeah, well *she* didn't help,' said Grey, looking at Bella.

Tara nodded. 'Yeah. Back at the church I thought it might have been Dude but here, no way. Whatever that thing was, it wasn't my Dude. He would never throw things around and freak me out like that.'

'So what do you want to do?' asked Jenni.

Tara stuck her head back round the door and surveyed the scene. 'Get rid of it. This is my bedroom. I have to *sleep* in here tonight and I don't want anything horrible hanging about.'

'So let's get a ghostbuster,' said Jenni.

'Oh, get real Jen. I've seen "Ghostbusters", but excuse me, where are we going to find one? In the Yellow Pages? I don't think so.'

Jenni shook her head. 'Nah. There's this boy at my school. He's a bit of a creep, in year eleven, but I think he may be able to help.'

'Oh, yeah,' nodded Tara. 'How?'

'Ghosts are his thing. He says he can get rid of them. He did an article for our school mag about it last year. Fancies himself as a ghostbuster. We used to think he was bonkers ...'

'He sounds bonkers,' said Tara.

'No, hear me out,' continued Jenni. 'I'm trying to help. We all used to laugh at him until Mrs Young down our road thought she had a ghost. Sid Wiper sorted it and she was never bothered again. Honest. Ask my mum.'

Dude rolled his eyeballs and began to laugh. 'Oh, right. A creep from Jenni's school. Hit me, Sid ...'

But Bella and Grey weren't laughing with him. Their faces had dropped and Grey looked seriously worried.

'Sid Wiper,' Grey said to Bella. 'Now look what you've gone and done.'

Eight

'This is all we need,' sighed Bogus when they got back to Mrs Riley's house and filled Bogus in on what had happened. 'Nice one, Bella.'

'I said I'm sorry,' said Bella. 'I didn't mean to ...'

'You really caused a mess back there,' said Dude who was still angry at her antics. 'I *really* wanted to get through to Tara.'

Bella looked sheepish. 'Sorry sorry sorry ...' she whispered.

'So. Sid Wiper,' said Bogus.

'Sid Viper more like,' said Grey as Bogus pulled his chair up to his computer and started tapping on the keyboard.

After a few minutes, he pushed his chair back. 'He's been after us for ages.'

'After you? Why?' asked Dude. 'Will someone please explain to me what is going on? Who is this kid?'

'He's not only after us. He's after all ghosts. He fancies himself as an amateur ghostbuster,' answered Bogus. 'Unfortunately, he's demonstrated a certain talent for it. Causes chaos on our level. Want to take a look at him, Dude?'

Dude nodded and moved closer to the screen as Bogus's fingers danced over the key-board. Up before them came a sour-faced youth. His almost shaven head made him look like a potato, and his tightly puckered mouth resembled a cat's bottom.

'Yeah, he looks like a team player. Not.' said Dude. 'Actually, he looks like he swallowed a lemon.'

'And that's him looking happy,' said Bogus. 'So that's Sid. Aged sixteen, and very dangerous. Had a bad experience once with a ghost when he was twelve.'

'It was Brazil,' said Bella.

'Brazil?' asked Dude.

'Brazil's another ghost. An old-timer. Brazil is his nickname so given because he's nuts. He likes to mess around. Bit of a poltergeist, I suppose you do know what one of them is?'

Dude nodded. 'Yeah. 'Course. A ghost who likes to throw stuff around.'

'Brazil's forte. He really likes freaking people out. Sid had the pleasure of his acquaintance on his twelfth birthday when Brazil managed to slip into Sid's birthday present.'

'It was a bike,' said Bella.'

'Yeah,' continued Bogus. 'He'd pestered his mum and dad for one for months. Then finally, the big day came and being a spoilt brat, he got exactly what he wanted. A beauty, red and silver number with loads of gears. Real flash, you know the kind. There it was all tied up in gold paper. As you can imagine, he couldn't wait to get on it. He ripped off the paper, leapt on the saddle and he was away. What he didn't know was that Brazil had hitched a ride. He went right up the bedroom wall, across the ceiling, down the banister, twice round the kitchen and out into the garden. His dad found him on the garage roof, white as a sheet and trembling like a jelly. Had to call the fire service out. Never did get on a bike again.'

'And since then,' said Grey, 'Sid's made it his life's mission to wipe out ghosts.'

'But how?' asked Dude. 'What can he do?'

'Plenty. All the information he needs is at his fingertips,' said Bogus, as he continued tapping on his key-board. 'This is bad, really bad.'

Bella and Grey stood behind him at the desk and looked anxiously at what he was doing.

'Has he got anyone yet?' asked Bella.

'Two that we know of. Jade the Slade and Howie Wails. Gone. They must have been surfing the Net this morning. I'm going to have to go in,' said Bogus gravely.

'No, *no*, you can't risk it,' cried Bella. 'It's too dangerous.'

'I'm lost again,' complained Dude. 'Go in where?'

'You explain, Bogus,' said Grey.

Bogus sighed wearily. 'You know anything about computers, Dude?'

Dude nodded. 'I had an Apple G4. Surfed the Net all the time.'

'Ever seen what an e-mail looks like?'

'Yeah, everyone has. Like a letter ... words.'

'Yeah,' said Bogus, 'but do you know how it's sent?'

'Um. Some kind of code isn't it?'

Bogus nodded. 'Ever seen what it looks like in code?'

Dude shook his head. 'Can't say ...'

'Every message, image and text is converted into code when it's sent,' said Bogus, pressing a key on the computer. 'Usually html. I'll show you. See this image?'

Dude nodded as an image of two hands shaking appeared on the screen.

'OK, example,' said Bogus. 'Every image, every message that appears on the screen is converted into it's own individual code. With me so far?'

Dude nodded. He wasn't quite sure what Bogus was on

about but he wasn't going to let him think he was thick. 'Yeah, code … cool.'

Bogus pressed another key and a page of what looked like gobbledygook appeared on screen, lines of letters and symbols that made no sense at all.

```
GIF89ak  9  ˜Ω  3(((333  f33fb}10z88PPPz@@fffxxx
ô33ô  Ã  ˇ33Ã33ˇffôffÃff˘îÜ##à88ì((ë88ò00•≤µ∞∏•
†((®((†88∞∞((∏∏((∞00∞88∫00ÑHHè@@ÉZZìHHèPPê\\
òXXázzíjjò``¨ïzz¢@@£HH†PP†]]®PP®]]¥@@¥HH≤PP¥XX†
hh®hh†pp†xx®pp®zz∂``≤hh∞pp≤xx¿  ¿»  »¿¿»»»–  –ÿ
ÿ—ÿÿ¿  ¿((»  Œ((À00À<<ÿ  ÿ((‡  ‡Ë  Ë‡Ë?  ˆ˘  ?_Ú‡
ÏË((¿HH≈XXflCC\\√jj≈xx÷jjôôfîååôôô†ÄÄ†àà®àà†êê†ú
ú®êê®òò∞ÄÄ∞àà∏ÄÄ∏àà∞êêµòò∏êê†††®††®®®∞
††∞®®∏∏††∏®®∞∞∞∏∞∞∏∏∏ôôÃôô˘∆ÄÄ»àà¿êê∕ÇÇ
'ëê¿††ƒ®®»††¿∞∞¿∏∏Õ∞∞∞÷®®›µµÏº∏ÃÃô»¿¥˘˘ô¿¿¿
»¿¿»»»ÃÃÃ–¿¿–»»fi¿¿ÿ»»——ÿ—ÿÿÿAĀ˘‡»»‡—‡ÿÿËÿÿ˘˘˘
Ã‡‡‡Ë‡‡ËËË?Ë
```

'That's what the image of the two hands looks like in code. And there are about twenty-five pages of it. Now watch this. I'm going to delete one letter from the first line of the code.' He pressed a key and a letter disappeared from line one. 'Now the rest of the code is there minus one letter, yeah?'

'Yeah,' said Dude.

Bogus pressed another key and the screen went blank. 'Wiped. See, the image of the hands is no more. You remove one tiny element of the code and bingo, you've corrupted it, the image is no more. Gone.'

'Yeah,' said Dude, feeling none the wiser. 'But what has a lesson in how e-mails are sent got to do with Sid's ghost-zapping antics.'

'There's a lot of ghosts on the Net,' said Bogus. '24-7. Hundreds, thousands of them are surfing all over the world.'

'Oh, yeah,' said Dude, 'Grey said you liked to surf.'

'Exactly. And that's how we travel, as code along the Net. It's fast and usually safe. Each one of us has our own unique code but there are elements that we all have in common. And there's the problem. The elements that identify us as ghosts. Now Sid is an ace hacker. Really knows his stuff. He was into breaking codes long before he was a ghostbuster. When he did a search on ghosts, he came across a surfing ghost's code stream and that was it. He soon identified the elements that every ghost has in common in his code. He deletes that and if you happen to be on the Net when Sid's in attack mood, bingo, you're gone. Understand?'

'Um. Sort of,' said Dude.

'Best if you show him, Bogus,' said Bella.

Bogus nodded to Grey who picked up a digital hand scanner.

'I'm going to scan Bogus in,' he said, as he began to trace Bogus's outline with the scanner.

Dude watched with amazement as Bogus started to disappear. A minute later his jaw fell open, as there was Bogus waving from the computer screen.

'You have to be very still at the moment when you're scanned in,' explained Bella, 'so that no part's missed out. Then, once you're in, you can go anywhere.'

A voice came through the computer. 'Now show Dude what I look like in code.'

Grey pressed a key on the computer and Bogus's image disappeared as the screen filled with incomprehensible writing and symbols. 'That's Bogus in code. See now? If I was to delete only one of those letters and symbols, Bogus is gone.'

Dude nodded. 'Holy *Moley*. So that's what Sid's doing.

He's deleting ghosts on the Net.'

'Exactly. Sid's developed a virus that tracks down the ghost code on the Net. The virus is very clever as it only wipes the symbols of the code that identifies ghosts. It's lethal to us,' said Bella.

'A virus. I hate the sad plonkers who do that. Messes everything up,' said Dude.

'Exactly,' said Bella. 'Now come out of there, Bogus, before Sid wipes you out. She pressed the key to change the code back into Bogus's image then pressed print. The printer whirred into action and out floated Bogus.

'Get it now?' he asked.

'Respect,' said Dude. 'I get it.'

'So you understand how bad this is for us?'

Dude nodded. 'But if we don't go in, we're OK, yeah?'

'Well, yeah,' said Grey, 'but what about all those who are *already* in? We have to stop Sid's virus or change the ghost code again, before he gets to them.'

'Yeah, what about the others, the ones he's already got to?' asked Dude.

Bogus glanced at Bella. 'That's why I want to go in. I've been working on this for weeks. I e-mailed out and got every ghost who has ever been on the Net to send me their code. I have them all on file on CD. *All* of them. Hector's made it into one of the new rules. No one can go on the Net without registering with me first so when someone goes missing, I can go in, duplicate their code and replace the elements Sid wiped out. Plus, I've been working on some anti-virus software to stop him reaching us, but it's taking time. In the meantime, all I can do is update the ghost element of the code daily, so we're always one step ahead of Sid. Sadly for us, it's his passion and he seems to have all the time in the world to try and keep up with us.'

'So that's why you've had your nose stuck in the computer for weeks,' said Grey.

'Yup,' said Bogus. 'But Bella's right. Sid might wipe me out before I can do anything. And it's a bit risky, as you guys might not be able to access the files where I've got all the codes stored, mine included. It's pretty complicated.'

'No way I could do it,' said Grey. 'I don't understand half of it.'

'We should go and pay him a visit,' said Dude.

Bogus shook his head. 'Don't want to agitate him more than necessary. He's pretty tuned in to when one of us is around. It may spook him into a panic and then who knows what he might do.'

'What we need,' said Dude, 'is someone to go and crash his computer.'

'Good idea,' said Bogus, looking at Dude with admiration. 'It will stop him, at least for the time being, and then I could go in and rescue the others. Yeah, but we need a live dude to get round there.'

'How about Mrs Riley?' suggested Grey.

'Nah,' said Bogus, shaking his head. 'She couldn't tell a computer from a gas cooker. We need someone who knows what to do.'

'Liam,' said Dude. 'My kid brother. He knows about computers. And he's always believed in ghosts. He'll be perfect.'

Nine

It was past midnight by the time the Dead Dudes arrived at the Harris house. All was quiet, as they slipped through the front door and up to Liam's bedroom, where Dude was surprised to find his brother still awake. He was lying on his bed listening to a CD through headphones. Dude was touched to see that it was Dirty Laundry's first recording, and Liam looked tearful. Dude longed to reach out and give him a hug but he'd learnt a lot in his short time as a ghost. He didn't want to frighten him.

'So how do we go about this?' asked Dude, hovering at the door.

'Umm, let me think,' said Bogus, looking round the room. 'We need him to hear you but first he has to will it. Above all, we mustn't scare him. First let him know that you're here. Try touching him.'

Dude reached out. Octopuses he thought, bits glued together, heavy, my hand is solid. He touched Liam's hand but as in the church with Tara, Liam leapt back in terror.

'Whas*sat*?' he cried.

Dude heard movement next door then his mum's bleary-eyed face looked round the door. 'You all right, Liam? I thought I heard something.'

'That's blown it,' said Dude. 'We're going to scare the living daylights out of them.'

'I'm fine, Mum,' said Liam. 'Just listening to one of Dude's CDs that's all. Must have sung along out loud.'

'Now come on, love,' said Mo. 'Time to put your

Walkman away. It's late. Try and get some sleep.'

As she gently closed the door behind her, the ghosts looked at each other warily

'What now?' asked Dude.

Before anyone could answer, Liam sat up on the bed and looked round the room. 'Dude,' he whispered. 'That you?'

'Hey, cool kid, he's willing to talk to you, Dude,' said Bella. 'Say something.'

'Hey, Liam,' said Dude. 'Can you hear me?'

Liam went very white but he nodded his head. 'Where are you?'

Dude sat next to him on the bed. 'Right here beside you. On the bed.'

'You a ghost?'

'Sure am,' said Dude. 'Hundred percento a Dead Dude.'

'What's it like?'

'Kinda weird, but I'm getting used to it.'

'Awesome,' said Liam. 'Why can't I see you?'

'Dunno mate. Hey, Grey, why can't he see me?'

'Grey, who's Grey?' asked Liam looking scared again.

'Tell him that seeing us takes time, he might be able to one day,' said Grey.

'Grey's my … my new mate, don't worry, he's OK,' chuckled Dude. 'He says it takes time but he says you might be able to one day.'

'This Grey, he's here too?'

'Yeah, in fact there's four of us here.'

'*Four?* Whoa, is that cool or what? Can I talk to them?'

'Yeah,' said Dude. 'You have to will it though. Bit like vampires in those films we used to watch on telly – they can only go into a house if they're invited. Same with us,

76

you have to will to hear us. Most people are too spooked because they think ghosts are scary – but they're not, some of them are really ... um ... normal.'

Liam took a deep breath, looked around the room and up at the ceiling. 'So, who's here?'

'There's Grey, he's my guide ... sort of, Bogus, he's a computer whiz, and Bella.'

'A girl ghost?'

'Yeah,' he said, then leant over and whispered into Liam's ear. 'And between you and me, she's a bit of babe. You can shake hands with them if you like.'

'Excellent,' said Liam, putting his hand out. 'Pleased to meet you all, I'm sure.'

Dude felt very proud of his little brother as each of the ghosts stepped forward and shook hands.

'Kind of cold,' said Liam. 'But it's amazing. I can feel you. I wish I could see you.'

'Turn off the light, Liam,' said Bogus. 'We could try something.'

Liam did as he was told and groped his way back to the bed through the dark.

'OK, I'm over by the wardrobe,' said Bogus. 'Now half close your eyes – try not to be frightened, we don't look weird. Then be very still and tell me what you see.'

Again Liam did as he was told. 'I see, I see ... it's very dark, no, hey, I see like a ... shimmery light ...'

'Keep concentrating Liam,' said Bogus. 'You're doing really well. We can be seen but you have to tune in. Imagine your mind's like a radio and you're tuning it one hundred percent to this room. Take a few deep breaths and keep real calm.'

Dude, Grey, and Bella went and stood next to Bogus as Liam strained to see.

'I can see more light now, shimmery, bluey-white, and hey, ohmigod, *ohmigod*, Dude,' Liam's eyes filled with tears. 'I can see you, I can *see* you … ohmigod….' Liam rushed forward to hug Dude but his arms went straight through him and he collided with the wardrobe door.

Once again, there was movement from next door.

'Mum's coming back,' said Dude. 'Don't say anything.'

Mo Harris put her head round the door. 'Liam, I thought I told you to go to sleep.'

'Sorry Mum,' he said. 'Going now. Just getting … I was just getting…'

'A pair of socks,' whispered Dude.

'A pair of socks,' said Liam. 'My feet are cold.'

'OK, then settle down, OK? We've all had a long day.'

'OK, Mum,' said Liam, as Mo closed the door behind her.

'Phew,' said Liam, turning back to the ghosts. 'This is *so* cool. I can see all of you now. Bogus, Grey, and hey, Bella …' Liam turned to Dude and winked. 'See what you mean about the babe ghost. And cool outfit.'

'Thing is, Liam,' said Bogus, stepping forward. 'We need your help …' and quickly he filled him in on their predicament.

Liam nodded his head as he listened. 'What a creep,' he said when Bogus had finished. 'Crash his computer. No prob. But I can't go now. Mum will hear.'

'Tomorrow,' said Grey. 'We'll go tomorrow morning.'

Liam looked sad. 'You going to leave again Dude?'

Dude shook his head. 'Nah. You go to sleep and we'll sleep in my old room.'

'You *sleep*?'

'D'oh, yeah, of course,' grinned Dude. 'Or should I say of corpse.'

Grey started giggling. 'Of corpse ... now why didn't I think of that.'

Dude went to the door. 'See you in the morning, kid.'

'Night Dude,' said Liam as he settled down in his bed.

'Night Liam,' said Dude.

'Night Liam,' said Bella.

'Night Bella,' said Grey.

'Night Bella,' said Bogus.

'Night Bogus,' said Bella.

'Night Dude,' said Grey.

'Night Grey Boy,' said Dude.

Ten

The next morning after Liam had set himself up with a triple Weetabix, and the Dead Dudes had had a good sniff of toast and hot chocolate, the group set off for Sid's.

'So what's the plan?' said Liam when they reached the corner of Sid's street.

'Knock on the door, ask to see Sid,' said Bogus, 'Then tell him you've heard that he's the main man when it comes to ghostbusting. Tell him you hate ghosts and you've got a problem that needs his top class help. Play to his ego.'

'Right,' said Liam, setting off. 'No 19 with the red door?'

'That's it, kid,' said Dude. 'And we'll be right behind you, but don't let on.'

Mrs Wiper answered the door. A great bulldog of a woman with a wispy moustache and legs like a rugby player. 'Sid, it's for you,' she barked up the stairs, then disappeared into the kitchen.

A moment later, Sid appeared in the hall. 'What do you want?' he growled.

'N ... need your help,' stuttered Liam. 'G ... got a problem.'

'So?' sneered Sid. 'Most of the planet's got a problem but they're not knocking on my door.'

'Heard you were into, least ... not into, against ... anti, don't like ... detest in fact ... you're exceptional ... only one.'

'Spit it out, squirt,' said Sid impatiently. 'Need my help for what?'

'Ghosts.'

'*Shhhhh*,' whispered Sid as his mother reappeared behind him. 'Don't *say* that word here.'

'Just going out to the shops,' said Mrs Wiper. 'Want anything?'

'Nah. Yeah. Ice-cream,' he said, as she went out the door. 'And some chocolate and crisps. Oh, and a few cans of Coke.'

He glanced up and down the street as his mother disappeared round a corner, then beckoned Liam in and indicated that he should follow him up the stairs.

Liam did as he was told with a brief look behind to check that the Dead Dudes were with him. Dude gave him the thumbs up.

Once inside his bedroom, Sid relaxed, but the dudes looked like they were in trouble.

'Woahhhhhh, *phoorrr*,' said Dude, falling back against the wall as all the ghosts put their fingers over their noses.

'Garlic,' said Bogus, as he surveyed the dingy room and spotted strings of garlic hanging above Sid's bed. 'He's seen too many vampire films. Suppose he thinks it keeps us away.'

'Might just work,' said Dude faintly, and stuck the nose-plugs Grey had given him up his nostrils.

'And if garlic doesn't, his socks will,' groaned Bella. 'This is one stinky kid. This room smells like ... a ton of pickled onions ...'

'And a vindaloo curry botty burp,' moaned Grey.

'And boiled school cabbage,' said Bogus.

Bella collapsed back on the bed. 'He doesn't need to worry about wiping us out on the Net ... he only needs to get us into this room.'

'Liam, try and get him to open the window,' whispered Dude.

'Phew, it's hot in here,' said Liam. 'Any chance of opening a window?'

Sid ignored his request. 'Right,' he said, eyeing Liam with the kind of look most people have when they see a delicious meal. 'You were saying. Ghosts?'

'Um, yeah,' said Liam. 'I heard you knew all about them.'

'I do indeed,' said Sid. 'Must be eradicated from the face of the earth ... evil, nasty, horrible, creepy...'

It was then that Liam spotted Dude with the plugs up his nose, and before he could stop himself, he burst out laughing.

Sid whirled round in the direction of Dude. 'What? *What?* You seen something? Why you laughing? Is there something here?'

Liam shook his head and tried to look serious. 'Bit nervous that's all. You know, g ... ghosts, s ... scary.'

Sid seemed appeased. 'Well, yeah, that's understandable. Ghosts are really heavy business.'

'Ask how he wipes them out,' whispered Bogus.

'So how do you deal with them?' said Liam. 'I hear that you're the best ...'

But Sid had gone rigid and was surveying the room with half-closed eyes. 'There's something in here. Something followed you in,' he snarled.

'He's rumbled us,' said Dude.

'We're done for,' said Grey.

Sid pushed Liam aside and sprang into action. 'Out of my way, snotrag, we got company ... nasty slimy company ...'

82

The Dead Dudes shrank against a wall as Sid threw himself into a chair in front of his computer in the corner of the room. He punched the start button with one hand and seized his scanner with the other. Liam raced over to the wall and stood in front of the ghosts, puffing himself out as far as he could to protect them.

'You leave them alone with that,' he warned.

'*Them*, huh?' retorted Sid. 'You devious little toe-rag. So there's more than one creepy-crawler here.'

Liam cried out as Sid aimed his scanner behind him. Bella disappeared and reappeared on the computer screen behind Sid.

'Help,' she mouthed from her electronic cage.

'Ha! Got one,' cried Sid. 'Now who wants the same treatment?'

Dude floated up to the ceiling when he saw that Sid was scanning with wild abandon. Sid shoved Liam aside and scanned in the area behind and around him. Dude watched in horror as Bogus and Grey dove aside like football players. Bogus flung himself into a corner but too late, the scanner found him and he was zapped onto the screen.

'Under the bed,' cried Dude to Grey.

Grey made a dive towards the bed while Sid went berserk with his techno sabre, scanning everything, going into his cupboard, under the computer desk, over the door.

He stopped for a moment, looked around, then fixed a stony stare at the bed. 'Now one of you wouldn't by any chance be under there, *would* you?' he cried as he leapt over to the bed and aimed his scanner underneath. Grey's legs disappeared, then his arms, followed by his torso, and finally his head.

Sid whirled round to look at the screen. 'Hah, got you,'

he cried triumphantly, as he viewed the three of them cowering in a corner of the screen. 'Any others out there?' he cried, as he aimed his scanner round the walls one last time.

'No, that's all of them,' Liam gulped.

'Good,' said Sid, licking his lips. 'Now. Say good-bye ghosties.' He pulled his key-board closer to him and wiggled his fingers at the screen. 'Time to enter the oblivion code.'

'*DO* something Liam,' cried Dude from the ceiling.

Liam sprang into action and threw himself at Sid knocking him clean off his chair. 'That's for Grey,' he cried.

'*Timber*,' mouthed Grey, going into boxing mode on the screen. 'Attaboy, Liam. Get him.'

Cursing mightily, Sid tried to get to his feet but Liam was onto him. 'That's for Bogus,' he said, twisting Sid's left ear.

Sid crashed his fist into Liam's nose and Liam reeled back in shock. He ducked out of the way narrowly missing an elbow in the eye as Sid attempted to get up and reach his desk. Quick as a flash, Liam rugby-tackled him back onto the floor. 'And that's for Bella.'

From up above, Dude noticed that Bogus was frantically gesturing from the screen. He had his hand up to his ear and was trying to say something Dude couldn't hear.

'Audio, audio,' mouthed Bogus.

'But won't he hear you?' asked Dude, as he floated down to the computer.

Bogus shook his head as Dude made his hand go solid and punched the audio key.

'Nah,' said Bogus. 'He doesn't know everything about ghosts and has to consciously will to hear us. Besides all bullies are cowards underneath. His fear's blocking his will. Now print us out.'

'He doesn't look very frightened to me,' said Dude, as the grappling pair behind him crashed about on the floor.

'Come *on* Dude, *hurry*,' urged Bogus.

Dude searched for the printer button and leant in to turn it on, when he heard Bella shout. 'Watch *out*!' Liam reeled into the desk as Sid's fist came up and gave him a nasty smack on the jaw. The monitor rocked perilously as Liam and Sid pounded each other around the carpet. Again they fell against the desk and the printer wobbled then fell onto the floor, the connecting cable flying loose.

Sid's face was red and sweaty as he lunged for Liam. As they fought it out on the floor, Liam's lack of size began to tell. Sid was bigger than him, and when Sid went for his throat with meaty hands, Liam started to show signs of weakening.

Dude couldn't take any more. He was about to will both his hands to be solid and give Sid an almighty thwack but Bogus saw him and called out from the screen. *'Don't*, Dude. Don't let him know that you're here or else he may zap you as well.'

'But I have to do *something*,' cried Dude. 'Liam's taking a beating.' He dove for the printer in an attempt to reconnect it.

'*Too* risky, Dude,' called Bogus. 'He might see.'

'Put his pants on his head, Liam,' urged Bella pointing out of the screen, 'On the floor, over there, his underpants...'

'Choose your weapons, men,' chortled Grey. 'Swords or Y-fronts.'

Bogus whacked him. 'This is *serious*, Grey.'

As Liam wriggled underneath Sid, he spotted a pair of droopy underpants on the floor by the bed. He looked desperately for something else but he couldn't see anything on the floor apart from carpet fluff, old tissues, discarded pizza boxes, and empty coke cans.

Sid was heading for the computer again when, with an almighty yank, Liam pulled him back onto the floor.

'Leave them alone, spudhead,' he cried.

On screen, the Dead Dudes cheered but Sid had already staggered back up.

'You can do it, Liam,' called Dude. 'Go for the pants.'

Liam reached out for the Y-fronts with a look of disgust. With one swift movement, he had them over Sid's head.

'Ar*gghhhh*,' cried Sid his strength suddenly weakening as he fell. 'Hor*rible* smell.'

'You said it,' said Liam, as he sat on Sid's chest and put his knees on Sid's elbows. 'Now you leave those ghosts alone. Not all of them are bad, you know.'

At last, Dude saw an opportunity to help Liam. He willed his hands to go solid and joined his little brother, pulling Sid's hair and twisting his ears.

'Oof, aafff. My ghosts, they're my ghosts now,' came Sid's muffled voice as he struggled to get Liam off him.

The Dead Dudes peered out of the screen as the boys wriggled and writhed on the floor in front of them.

'We've got to get out of here,' said Bogus. 'Liam, keep him down there.'

'Belt, Dude,' said Grey, pointing with his finger out of the screen. 'On the end of the bed.'

As Liam continued to kneel on Sid, Dude reached out for the belt. He quickly wrapped it round Sid's ankles as Sid struggled with all his might.

Next, Liam whipped off his own belt, then grabbed Sid's wrists and tied them as tightly as he could. At last, Sid was sorted. He lay on the carpet writhing like a snake.

'Quick, Liam,' called Bogus. ''We've *got* to get out of

86

here before he gets free.'

'Yeah, right,' said Bella. 'And just how do you suggest we do that, seeing as we seem to be trapped on a *computer* screen. Train? Boat? Bus?'

'We'll take the Outlook Express,' said Bogus, 'Liam. Open it and send us somewhere. Quick.'

'*Where*? Where would you be safe?' asked Liam, standing over the screen.

'Back to Mrs Riley's,' suggested Dude. 'What's the address Bogus?'

'Spooksrus@spooky.every1.net,' said Bogus, 'And *hurry.*'

Sid had squirmed his way over to Liam's feet and was biting his ankles through the pants over his head. Liam desperately typed in the address while trying to kick Sid out of the way.

'You're doing great, Liam,' said Dude, as Sid took a particularly vicious bite at Liam's ankle as he located Grey on the desktop. Then Sid staggered up and surged heavily against him. Before Liam could move Bogus next to Grey, Sid fell forward onto the key pad. Liam's hand slipped and the 'send' beep sounded from the computer.

'Just keep calm and agghh ... help me I'm melting ...' Grey cried, as he faded then disappeared.

'*Ohmigod*,' cried Liam, shoving Sid back down, 'Grey's gone. I don't know what I pressed! I don't know where I sent him.'

'Oblivion, I hope,' muttered Sid through his pants as he continued to bite Liam's ankles.

Just get me back to Mrs Riley's,' called Bogus. 'Don't panic ... oh, *no*, Bella's done a runner. She's gone into Internet Explorer. Quick, Liam, GET ME HOME.'

'I'm *trying*,' cried Liam, beginning to lose it. He whirled round and kicked the grovelling Sid back onto the floor. 'Stay down, you jerk.'

But Sid didn't give up easily. He'd wriggled his hands free from the belt and whipped his pants off his head. He lurched forward at Liam, as he made a desperate attempt to send Bogus off.

Sid was shoving with all his strength, trying to push Liam away from the desk. However, his feet were still tied in the belt so he was having difficulty moving.

'What?' asked Liam, spotting that the wardrobe door was ajar. 'Hopping mad are you? Well *so* AM I.' With an almighty thrust, he pushed Sid back and after a few stumbling steps, he fell against the wardrobe. Liam opened the door and pushed Sid inside.

'See if you can find Narnia while you're in there,' he cried, as he turned the key in the lock.

He ran back to join Dude at the computer. 'Bogus, *Bogus*, you all right?'

Bogus nodded from the screen. 'Just get me home then crash the computer. All you need to do is open the My Computer icon, double-click on C drive, hold the CTRL key down on the key-board and click on the four icons, autoexec, autoexec.dos, command, and config.dos. That's it. Then delete, then close My Computer, right button click on Recycle Bin, choose "empty" and pull the plug.'

Liam frantically scribbled down the instructions on a pad on the desk then made sure Bogus was safely in an attachment to an e-mail bound for Mrs Riley's address, before pressing 'send'.

'See you back there, 33 Bardo Street,' called Bogus, as he too began to disappear from the screen. 'And don't forget to crash the computer ...'

'I will,' said Liam. 'Fast as I can.'

Inside the wardrobe, Sid pounded on the door and shouted defiantly.

'We haven't got long before he gets out,' said Dude. 'Quick, delete the address at Mrs Riley's then close Outlook Express.'

Liam did as he was told.

'Now open My Computer, double click on C drive, hold the CTRL key down on the key-board and click on the four icons, auto exec, autoexec. dos, command, and con fig.dos,' said Dude, reading the instructions. 'Then delete. Now close My Computer, right button click on Recycle Bin and choose "empty". Excellent. Now find the mains.'

Liam bent over the back of the desk. 'Here it is, Dude.'

'Now pull the plug,' instructed Dude.

The image of a bomb came up as the screen went blurry. Liam could just about make out the words, error. Your machine has … and the screen went blank.

'That should do it,' said Dude, heading for the door. 'Now stuff those instructions into your pocket, don't want Sid to find out what we've done, and let's get *out* of here.'

He and Liam raced down the stairs, out of the door, and legged it down the street.

Eleven

Liam was almost in tears by the time he and Dude reached Bardo Street.

'I'm *sooo* sorry I ... I sent Grey into ... oblivion,' he said, as he and Dude reached no 33. 'I'm gutted ... him being your guide and everything, your new dead mate...'

'Listen, Liam, it wasn't your fault,' said Dude, as he slid through the door. 'I'm sure he'd understand. We put Sid out of business for the time being and you saved the rest of us ... anyway, maybe Bogus will find Grey. That's if he's got back OK.'

Dude was halfway up the stairs when he heard a loud knock on the front door and a muffled shout from Liam.

He rushed back down to the door just as Mrs Riley let Liam in.

'You're not used to being back with mortals are you, Dude?' she smiled. 'You've forgotten that they can't walk through things like you can.'

'Sorry, Mrs R, I forgot ... lot on my mind. Meet my brother, Liam.'

'Hallo,' said Liam, staring intently at the old lady.

'Hallo, duck. Oh, don't worry, I'm not a ghost,' she said. 'Now come on in the kitchen. I bet you two are hungry.'

They trooped into the kitchen where Mrs Riley took the lid off a large pot and gave it a stir. 'Fancy a bit of chicken soup? Be ready soon.'

'Smells fab already,' said Dude.

'We'll give it a few more minutes,' she said, then looked around. 'Where's my Bogus?'

Dude looked uncomfortably at Liam.

'Come on, out with it,' said Mrs Riley.

'Um, we had a bit of a problem,' said Dude. 'I know this might sound stupid but we had a run in with mad Sid. And um, we had to e-mail Bogus back. He said to print him out.'

'Oh, stuck on the Net again is he? Honestly, that boy ...' To Dude's amazement, she didn't bat an eyelid. 'You know where his room is, don't you? You boys, all computer mad ... soup in ten minutes, OK?'

Dude and Liam sped up the stairs as fast as they could and burst into Bogus's room where Liam quickly powered up the computer.

Dude silently prayed that it had worked, when a familiar beep announced a message in the Inbox.

'We've got mail,' said Liam, as he hit the open key.

Much to their relief, there was Bogus waving from the screen.

'Phewww,' sighed Dude. 'Print him out quick.'

Moments later, Bogus floated into sight.

'Wow! Look at that! It worked.' said Liam. 'You OK?'

Bogus nodded then patted Liam on the back. 'Tough kid, your brother,' he said to Dude. 'He was great back there.'

Dude nodded and smiled at Liam. 'I was really proud of you. Especially when you did that thing with the Y-fronts.'

The three of them cracked up as Liam mimicked Sid stumbling about his room with his pants on his head.

'Anyway, we're safe for a while now, so best get Grey and Bella out,' said Bogus.

'But how will you know where they are?' asked Liam. 'I don't know where I sent them.'

'Bella went into Internet Explorer so I know *exactly* where she'll be.'

'Where?' asked Dude.

'In some teen chatroom. She loves them. It's one of the few places where she can yabber away and no one gets that she's a ghost.'

'Hey,' said Dude. 'I could go to *my* web site and chat to my fans.'

'Yeah, you could,' said Bogus. 'Like, that wouldn't draw much attention. Yeah, dead rock stars talking from beyond the grave. Happens all the time. The press would love it. Front pages even. Sid would be there in an instant and you, my stupid friend, would be Dead Dude history.'

'Oh, yeah,' said Dude. 'Der.'

'Do you know where Grey is as well?' asked Liam.

Bogus shook his head. 'Not exactly. But I'll find him.' He went to Directory Search on his index and rapidly punched in a few keys. 'Grey and I often surfed together as he didn't like to do it alone, so I've memorised his code. Won't take a minute.'

'How long do you think Sid's computer will be out of action?' asked Dude.

'Day or so at least,' replied Bogus. 'Unless Sid's a complete computer genius, he'll have to take it down the repair shop so maybe even a week before he's back up and running. He's good but I'm better. He's not …'

'Not the sharpest blade on the penknife,' replied Liam winking at Dude.

'Nor the brightest crayon in the pencil-box,' grinned Dude.

'Nor the coolest cube in the icebox,' said Liam.

'Nor …' began Dude.

'Cut it out, you two,' said Bogus, continuing his search. 'We haven't a moment to spare as there's always the possibility that Sid may have access to someone else's computer.'

'Sorry,' said Liam. 'Just … Dude always thought he was dead funny. Now he is.'

Bogus rolled his eyes and hit a few more keys on the computer. After a few moments, he gave them the thumbs up. 'Found him.'

'Where?' asked Dude. 'Where is he?'

'Down under,' grinned Bogus. You only e-mailed him to Australia, Liam! And, oh, oh … better get him out of there, real quick. Hold on.' Bogus pressed a few more keys and soon Grey was on screen looking rather shaken. A moment later, he floated out of the printer.

'Phew, that was a close call,' he wheezed and slumped down on Bogus's bed. 'Thank God you got me when you did, Bogus.'

'Why? What happened?' asked Dude.

'Ended up on some graphic designer's web site didn't I? Phew. Narrow escape.'

'Why?' asked Dude. 'What was the problem?'

'Graphic designer who designs *greetings* cards. He only pasted me into a Hallowe'en card. He was about to start rearranging my face, adding a few details to make me look spookier when Bogus pulled me out. Phew. I almost ended up like something from 'Nightmare on Elm Street'. It's enough to make you scream.' He let out his best graveyard ghoul wail.

Dude, Bogus, and Liam started laughing.

'Not funny,' said Grey.

'No, not funny at all,' said Dude, grinning from ear to

ear. 'Just glad to see you back in one piece, mate.'

'Hey, where's Bella?' asked Grey, looking around.

'Three guesses,' said Bogus.

'Chat-room?' said Grey.

Bogus nodded. 'Probably having the time of her after-life. But we'd better get her back in case Sid works a miracle recovery on his machine.'

He went to Internet Explorer and typed in www.chulochat.com. He punched in his user name then password and up on the screen came a list of chat-rooms available.

Dude leant over his shoulder. 'There's so many. How do you know which one she's in?'

'This time you've got the three guesses,' said Bogus.

Dude scanned down the list.

Chulochat! Rooms

American Teens – for USA flavoured chat.

Asian Teens – a place to meet new pals.

Beauty – the place for tip top beauticious tips

Date City – for the do's and don'ts of the dating game

Europe Teens – for European flavoured chat.

Goth City – for teens into the Goth scene

Health – everything you need to know but are afraid to ask

Love and Stuff – chat about your relationship

Music Mania – chat about your fave bands

Teen Advice Line – for the low down on love, school, family or friends

Shopping Mall – a place to cruise and hang out with pals.

Your Point of View – let's have those opinions!

Wonderful World – meet teens the world over, wherever, whatever

'Ah, got it,' grinned Dude. 'Goth City?'

'In one,' said Bogus, pressing the icon for Goth City.

On the screen, the script of dialogue came up on the left, and on the right the participants in the room.

'What seriously weird names,' said Liam, reading the list out. 'Bog-eye. The Protector. Black Sab. Shadowchaser. PrinceofGhoul. SadSadie. Crystalgaze. Gothmoth. Ah there she is. BellaGhostie.'

'What's she been saying?' asked Dude looking over Bogus's left shoulder.

'Take a look,' said Bogus, sliding over to make room for him.

Dude read the dialogue out loud.

'BellaGhostie: I feel invisible. It's so good to have someone to talk to.

PrinceofGhoul: Why what's your problem? Bad breath?

Bella: No one understands me and sometimes I feel that I'm not like other people.'

Grey chuckled. 'I reckon it's time to join in,' he said.

Bogus nodded and typed in a line.

'Here we go,' said Dude. 'Bardo, that your user name?'

Bogus nodded as Dude continued to read.

Bardo: Time to come home Bella.

'Look, someone's replying,' said Dude.

SadSadie: Who's that? Your dad? Look out, old man in the room.

Bella: No, but he thinks he is sometimes. Bog off, Bogus.

SadSadie : Yeah, get lost, saddo.

Bardo: It's not safe in there, Bella. I've warned you.

SadSadie : Don't go, Bella. Sounds like this Bardo isn't safe. I like you, I can really relate to that stuff about being invisible.

Bella: As if, Sadie. Beam me up, Scottie.

Bardo: Go to the Desktop, Bella.

PrinceofGhoul: What's going on?

Bella: I'm going onto another plane.

Bogus pressed 'print' and out floated Bella.

'I see we all made it,' she grinned, looking round the room. 'That was fun.'

'I don't think any of you realise how serious this is. It's not a game,' said Bogus. 'We all made it for now but Sid will be back and probably nastier than ever. He has to be stopped. Anyone got any brilliant ideas?'

Bella shrugged. 'We could crash his computer for good?'

Bogus shook his head. 'Too risky for us to go there again. And he'll never let Liam in again. Besides computers can be mended, hard drives can be replaced. We have to think of another way of stopping him'

'I've got a plan,' said Liam.

'What?' asked Bogus.

Liam looked anxiously at Dude. 'Tara,' he said.

'What about Tara?' asked Dude.

'I could tell her that I've seen Dude and he needs her help. She could pay Sid a visit. She's such a babe, Sid's bound to let her in.'

'What do you think, Dude?' asked Bogus.

'Phfff. She won't help,' pouted Bella. 'Remember what she was like when we paid her a visit before? She's such a pathetic scaredy-cat.'

'No she's not,' said Liam. 'She's really cool. For a girl that is.'

'Yeah,' said Dude. ' And I'd have thought you've done enough damage where Tara is concerned, so butt out, Bella. Yeah. It *is* a possibility if we could only get through to her. She can be a good sport when she wants to be. Yeah. Let's go.'

'It will be a waste of time,' Bella objected, as everyone stood up ready to leave. 'We don't need her.'

'We don't need *you*,' said Dude, giving her a dirty look.

'You stay here, Bella,' said Bogus. 'We're not risking letting you loose on her again.'

'Aw, come on. Promise I'll behave,' she said with an innocent smile.

'Yeah, right. And I wonder why I don't believe you?' said Bogus. 'In fact, I'll stay with you to make sure. I've got to go back into the Net anyway to replace the code missing on Jade the Shade and Howie Wails from the inside. I'll need you here to print me out after I've got them.'

Bella sat on the bed and looked miserable. 'You never let me have any fun,' she moaned.

'So deal with it,' said Bogus. 'Go on lads. Good luck and take care out there. It's a matter of death and death.'

Twelve

Dude couldn't wait to see Tara so he got Liam to call her right away.

'She's not there,' he said, replacing the receiver. 'Her mum says she's gone to the mall to meet someone. Five o'clock outside Costas.'

'Brilliant, well done, Liam,' said Dude. 'Let's go early and cruise the shops.'

'Good plan,' said Grey, looking at the clock by Bogus's bed. 'That gives us an hour.'

'Wow! Off to the shops with ghosts. Cool,' said Liam, then grinned, 'or should I say ghoul?'

Dude was amazed to see when they got to the mall how many other ghosts had had the same idea. He decided not to tell Liam as, although by now he was used to Dude and his new mates, it might be a bit of a shock if he saw how many ghosts there were about *all* the time. They were everywhere, on their own and in groups, just like normal shoppers – only they were more relaxed and not in a frantic hurry like the live people. In the cafés, they were sniffing the inviting aromas of fresh croissants, warm do'nuts, gooey chocolate cakes, and a dozen different types of coffee. There were huddles of female ghosts at the cosmetic counters, trying the latest perfumes or inhaling scents at the candle counters when the assistants' backs were turned. All of them were generally mooching about enjoying the afternoon.

'There are hundreds here,' Dude whispered to Grey, as he neatly side-stepped a couple of very fat old ghosts trundling past them towards a nearby ice-cream stand.

'Yeah,' said Grey. 'This is a favourite haunt of ours. Come on, they've got thirty-six flavours over there.'

Liam bought a double-vanilla and pistachio cone as Dude and Grey hovered over the ice-cream counter inhaling deeply.

'Mmmm, try the strawberry cheesecake,' said Dude.

'And the pecan fudge,' said Grey. 'Yumbocious.'

'And try some of this mango surprise, it's … it's …' words evaded Dude as he took yet another sniff of essence of ice-cream perfection.

Outside an electric shop, they spotted a group of young ghosts excitedly watching a football match on TV.

'Who's playing?' asked Grey.

'Our team,' said one of the boy ghosts. 'The Wraith Rovers.'

Inside the shop, another group of ghosts waited until the shop assistants were busy with customers then, quick as a flash, they were trying out the latest computers and scanners. One ghost disappeared from the shop-floor and reappeared on the screen of a PC, where he waved and made faces at all his mates.

Grey flew into the shop. 'Cool it lads. Mad Sid's about,' he warned. 'He's been deleting like nobody's business. Better come out until things quieten down a bit.'

'Cheers, Grey,' said the boys.

Dude heard the printer chatter into action next to him and out popped the boy from the screen.

'We'll get Bogus to send you an e-mail when it's safe,' said Dude, looking around to check that none of the shoppers had spotted the printer in motion.

'Hey, aren't you Dude from Dirty Laundry?' said a short ghost with spiky hair and a battered leather jacket.

'Yeah,' said Dude, feeling chuffed that he'd been recognised.

'Hey, look, it's him,' he shouted to his mates. 'It's Dude. Hey. You seen yourself in the CD shop? Top man, congratulations.'

'Yeah, check it out,' said another of the boys, pointing to a music-store nearby.

Dude, Grey, and Liam sped along to the CD shop and to Dude's delight, he saw the window was filled with a huge 3D display of himself and Dirty Laundry. Underneath, in three foot high electric blue lettering, it said that the band's last album, 'All Washed Out' was number one in the charts.

'Straight to number one. *Excellent*,' said Dude and high fived Grey. He noticed a couple of girls in the queue for the till with one of his CDs in their hand. 'Should I offer to sign my autograph?'

Grey chuckled. 'Best not,' he said.

'It's weird,' said Dude. 'When I was alive, I used to get fed up with people recognising me all the time and I longed to be anonymous, you know ... invisible in a crowd ...'

'Got your wish then didn't you?' Grey grinned.

'Probably time to go and see if Tara's arrived yet,' said Liam, looking at his watch.

On the way over to the coffee shop, Dude noticed that outside some of the shops, there were ghosts standing guard like bouncers at a nightclub.

'What are they doing?' he asked.

Grey laughed. 'Look at what they're selling Dude. I told you the rules.'

Dude glanced in at the window and saw that the display was full of dummies wearing bras and pants. 'Oh I get it, lingerie shop.'

'Yeah,' said Grey. 'Like I said, we aren't allowed to go spying on girls in the changing rooms. The heavies'll be in the clothes shops too. They work for Hector to make sure no one goes in.'

'Hey, there's Tara,' said Liam, pointing at a table outside the coffee shop. 'And she's alone.'

'OK. Now stay cool, Dude, whatever happens,' said Grey, as they glided in her direction. 'We mustn't scare her this time.'

'No problemo,' said Dude, as he watched her look up and spot Liam.

'Hey, Liam,' she called.

Liam went over to join her and for a few moments, both of them looked awkward, as if they didn't know what to say.

'So, um, how are you?' Liam asked, finally.

Tara's eyes filled up. 'Oh you know ...'

'Yeah,' said Liam. 'I know ...'

'I ... I really miss him,' said Tara.

'But I'm *here*,' said Dude. Of course, she didn't hear him so he took a step towards her and spoke again, softly. 'I'm right here, Tara.'

'Dude,' warned Grey. 'Leave it to Liam.'

'Well it bugs me that she can't hear me. She's supposed to be my girlfriend so why doesn't she will to hear me like Liam did?'

'D'oh Dude, you forgetting the little episode with Bella? It's no wonder she doesn't will it. Don't take it so personally.'

'About Dude,' Liam started, as Dude settled on the chair

opposite Tara, 'And you missing him. Well, um, it's like, he's not as far away as you think. In fact, er, um, I ... he ... he's still around.'

Tara sighed heavily. 'Don't even go there Liam. I thought I felt him at the funeral. Thought someone touched me, but it was wishful thinking. It was some other thing. Some crazy mad, bad spirit. Me and Jen tried to reach Dude when we got back after the church but all that came through was some horrible spook. Freaked the living daylights out of us, so I've learnt my lesson. You don't mess with the other worlds. You don't know who may be around.'

Liam nodded at Dude. 'Too true,' he said. 'You don't.'

'Anyway,' continued Tara, 'Jenni rang a ghostbuster to make sure whatever it was doesn't come back.'

'But I saw him, Tara. I *saw* him.'

'Yeah, right,' said Tara. 'And the yeti lives in our fridge. Look, I know it's hard, we both loved him but we've got to let go now and accept that our Dude has really gone.'

'Tell her all she needs to do is keep calm and will to hear me,' urged Dude.

Before Liam could say anything, they were joined by a sleek, blonde boy dressed in an expensive looking sweater and neatly pressed jeans. The boy nodded expressionlessly at Liam, who nodded back.

'Oh, no,' moaned Dude. 'Ben Fisher. He's wetter than a haddock's boxer shorts. He was at my old school. And I bet I know exactly what he wants, the creep. He's been after Tara for years. In fact, what's she doing meeting him? Jeez. I've only been gone a few days.'

'Stay cool,' warned Grey, as Ben handed Tara a card and a bunch of freesias then moved to sit on the chair where Dude was.

'For your time of grief, Tara,' said Ben. 'I'm so sorry to

hear about your loss.'

'Yeah. I bet,' said Dude, getting up sharpish as Ben almost sat through him.

Tara took the flowers and read the card. 'Thanks, that's so sweet of you' she said, looking really sad.

Ben got up, went over to her, gave her a tissue then opened his arms. 'You need a big hug,' he said, enveloping Tara in his arms.

'Over my dead body,' cried Dude, stepping forward but, once again, Grey pulled him back.

'Chill, Dude,' he said, then chuckled. 'Over your dead body …'

Ben knelt down and looked into Tara's eyes. 'I just want you to know that I'm here for you …'

'Pass me the bucket,' groaned Dude. 'I think I'm going to hurl.'

'And if there's anything I can do …' he pulled Tara in close and looked as if he was moving in for a snog.

'Enough,' said Dude, willing his hands to be solid. He leapt forward, grabbed the remains of Liam's ice-cream cone and shoved it onto Ben's head.

Ben jumped up and whirled round to Liam. 'Hey … what the…'

Liam held his hands up. 'Never touched you,' he said.

'Then who did this?' squawked Ben as the ice-cream dripped down his face and onto his jumper. 'This is *cashmere …*'

'Oh no,' said Tara, her eyes widening in horror. 'Don't say it's following me.'

'What? What's following you?' asked Ben, as he dabbed down his sweater.

'*Dude,*' said Liam. 'I told you. It's our Dude.'

'But he's dead,' cried Ben looking around.

103

'Never heard of ghosts?' asked Liam, as Dude stood in front of Ben and tweaked his nose.

'I *told* you, Liam,' said Tara. 'It can't be our Dude. This is something bad. It's that *thing* again.'

'What's going on?' asked Ben, backing off. 'I just felt something. What thing? What are you talking about?'

Dude grimaced. 'Let's get rid of this creep.'

'OK,' said Grey. 'But it means breaking the rules a tiny bit.'

'What rules are you on about now?' asked Dude. 'You never told me about a rule like this. We touched Sid didn't we?'

'Yeah, but we had a reason there,' said Grey. 'That was for the good of the whole ghost community. We're not supposed to make contact just for fun or to spook people. Imagine if we could. For a start, it would be mayhem in this mall with some of the young ghosts having a laugh. So, no, we can't touch anyone unless we have a reason, an important message to convey. Unfinished business or something.'

'And this isn't unfinished business?' said Dude, glowering at Ben.

Grey thought for a moment then grinned at Dude. 'After you, sir,' he said, as Liam sat on the vacant chair and giggled.

Dude went and stood behind Ben and started tickling under his arms.

'Who*aaaaa*! Wassat?' cried Ben, as Grey joined in by blowing air in his face. 'There … there's something …'

A group of shoppers stared in amazement at the sight of Ben wriggling around as though he had a nest of ants in his pants.

'Oh, no,' said Tara, who looked as scared as Ben. 'Not again.'

'It's Dude,' giggled Liam. 'Doesn't like dirtbag here messing with his girl.'

By now, a group of passing ghosts had gathered to watch the fun. They all turned to look at Ben who was deathly pale with his ice-cream-coated hair standing on end. Ben opened his mouth to speak just as Dude delivered a well-aimed kick to his backside.

'Arrrghhh,' shrieked Ben, and ran off into the crowd.

'See you later,' called Liam, watching him race up the nearest escalator.

'Much later,' said Dude.

'What a creep,' said Liam when he'd gone.

'Is it still here?' whispered Tara. 'Can you feel anything?'

'I *told* you,' answered Liam. 'It's *Dude*. You don't need to be scared. He only flipped because he saw Ben moving in on you.'

'Oh Liam, will you *drop* that stuff,' cried Tara. 'I can't deal with it.'

'But it's *true* Tara. And it was Dude at the funeral. He even went back to your house afterwards to try and talk to you but this other ghost went as well. Bella. She's got a crush on Dude and is jealous of you, so she started throwing things around ...'

Tara stared at Liam as though he'd gone mad. 'Must stay calm,' she said out loud to herself. 'It's my own fault for messing with stuff that's dangerous. It's that thing from my bedroom the other day. It must be following me.'

'It's not a thing,' said Liam. 'It's *Dude*.'

She took a deep breath, stood up and took Liam by the shoulders. 'Listen. I know it's difficult. It is for both of us, but we mustn't get into this stuff on our own. It's too weird. We need to find out what this thing is that's following

105

me. We need a professional.'

'Oh, no, not Sid again,' sighed Grey.

'Not Sid Wiper,' Liam began, 'because…'

'No,' interrupted Tara. 'My Auntie Betty. She's a medium. We'll go to her and see if she can contact Dude and find out what this other entity is. We'll go in the morning. Will that make you happy?'

Liam looked over at Dude and Grey for confirmation.

Dude looked sulky. 'Don't like being called a thing.'

Grey nodded to Liam. 'Yeah, I think I know who she means. Auntie Betty. All the old-timers who can't use computers go to her. She's cool.'

'Yeah,' said Dude. 'If it means Tara might finally realise that I am not a thing, let's do it.'

Liam looked back at Tara. 'Dude says yeah.'

Tara shook her head sadly. 'I thought I was bad. Don't you know that Dude would never act so freaky, Liam? Never mind. We'll get to the bottom of it. Poor, poor Liam.' She pulled Liam forward and cradled his head to her chest. Liam grinned cheesily at Dude and Grey.

'Don't push it, Liam,' said Dude, but he smiled as he smacked his little brother lightly across the head.

Thirteen

Dude was feeling faint again. The next morning, he and Grey had sped round to Auntie Betty's to make sure that they were there before Liam and Tara arrived. Trouble was, Auntie B kept cats. Lots of cats. Twelve of them in total, the whole bungalow smelt musty from used cat litter, dried cat food, and tom-cat spray.

'Use your nose-plugs,' said Grey.

Dude shook his head. 'No way, man. What if Tara breaks through today and can actually see me. No, I was the King of Cool. I can't have her seeing me looking like Prince Pratt.'

Grey shrugged. 'Your choice.'

'Besides,' continued Dude, looking out the window, 'all the other ghosts can tell I'm a new boy if I wear them.'

'But you are a new boy.'

'I know. But I've seen all the novices walking round with their plugs in. It makes them look like they're wearing nasal diapers.'

'Suit yourself, machoman.' Grey chuckled and bent down to stroke a majestic ginger moggie that was circling his ankles.

'Hey, these guys can see us can't they?' said Dude, as a black cat on the window-sill looked at him and meowed.

'Yeah. Some cats can and Auntie Betty's are used to our lot coming in and out of the place.'

The black cat began to purr like an old bus as Dude tickled under its chin. 'Oh. Here's our Liam and Tara now,' said Dude, waving out of the window.

Grey gave them a wave as well. 'So what's the plan?' he asked.

Dude shrugged. 'I reckon it should be easy. Tara's coming here, so she should be open and willing to hear me. Aunt Betty or no Aunt Betty, I should get through today.'

They heard a knock on the door then Liam and Tara being let into the hall.

'Don't get your hopes up, Liam,' said Tara. 'These things don't always work.'

'Oh, I think we may get a result.' Liam smiled as he saw Grey and Dude coming out of the front room

'Too right,' said Dude. 'Actually I think Auntie B's already in session. It's amazing, there's a whole pile of people and ghosts in there waiting for a go.'

'Go on in,' said the thin old lady who'd opened the door, ushering Liam and Tara into a back room. 'Sit here and wait your turn. It may be sooner, it may be later, as sometimes we don't know who's here already or who's going to come through from the other side.'

There were six live people in the darkened room. They glanced up when Liam and Tara went in, then looked back at Auntie B who was sitting at a table in the centre of the room with her eyes closed and a cat draped around her neck. She was wearing a voluminous floral dress, a large velvet hat, and was swaying slightly from side to side.

'She looks bonkers,' said Dude.

'Nah. She's OK really. Better get in the queue,' said Grey, indicating the line of ghosts waiting for a turn to speak.

'Hey, there's that gorgeous black girl,' said Dude, pointing down the line. 'The one who we saw celebrating her deathday. Wasn't she one of the one's Bogus rescued from the Net?'

'Oh, yeah. Hey, Jade,' called Grey. 'You OK?'

Jade grinned and stepped out of the queue. 'Yoh, Grey. Yeah, I'm cool. Close call back there on the Net. Bogus told us all about Sid – major bummer – but yeah, Bogus worked his magic with the codes and got me and Howie out.'

'So, why are you here?' asked Grey.

'Thought I'd try something different. I know this is usually the method the wrinklies use for communicating,' said Jade, nodding her chin at all the old dears in the line, 'But no way I'm risking the Net until it's safe again. Besides, the main man's forbidden it. No more surfing until he gives the OK.'

'Look, Dude, he's here,' said Grey, pointing at a large middle-aged ghost with grey hair and a big white moustache, who gave them a nod. 'That's the one and only Hector the Spectre. I'll introduce you later, as it looks like it's his turn.'

Back on the seats, Tara began to look pale as Hector disappeared then started speaking through Betty.

'I've come to tell you that there is life beyond,' his voice boomed through Betty.

'Is that our Jack?' cried an elderly woman on the seats. 'It *sounds* like our Jack? Jack love, can you hear me? You left your teeth. I've put them on your grave for you in a glass of water.'

An old ghost at the end of the queue grinned a toothless grin. 'Wondered where they were,' he said to the lady ghost next to him.

'It's not Jack, it's *Hector*,' said Hector.

In the meantime, some of the ghosts at the front of the queue were growing restless.

'Stop pushing,' said Jade the Shade, as a young boy

ghost jostled her.

'Oh, drop dead,' said the boy.

All the ghosts fell about laughing, even Hector the Spectre who, unfortunately, was still in Auntie Betty.

Tara watched Auntie Betty's shoulders heaving up and down.

'What's so funny?' she asked.

'Oh ... nothing,' chortled Hector through Auntie B. 'Ahem. Just a private joke.'

'Well, I want to speak to Dude,' said Tara, who was looking more than a bit freaked out.

'Anyone called Dude back there?' called Hector, out of Auntie Betty's right ear.

Dude stepped forward. 'Me. Me. I'm Dude.'

'Young lady here wants a word,' said Hector.

'Hey, I was next,' said an old lady ghost. 'Get back in line.'

Dude watched Hector slip out of the side of Betty's head. 'Give the boy a break,' he said to the old lady. 'He's new and it looks like his girl has come to have a say.'

Then he put his hand out to Dude and they shook hands.

'I've got my eye on you,' Hector said, removing an eyeball from its left socket and placing it on Dude's shoulder. Then he guffawed at Dude's look of horror. 'Hah, gets them every time. But you make sure you watch your step lad. And any problems, come to me.'

'Oh, I will, sir,' said Dude, handing Hector back his eyeball.

'He does that to all the new ghosts,' whispered Grey, coming up behind Dude. 'He's all right really.'

'But how did he do that?' asked Dude. 'Did he have a glass eye or something before he died?'

110

'Nah,' said Grey. 'It's the kind of advanced stuff that you'll learn later. It's like I was telling you before, everything is made up of energy. Energy vibrating in particular molecular constructions gives things different shapes and forms. It's physics really. As you learn more about it you can do almost anything. Take a leg off and wave it in the air, if you want. It's all a question of disconnecting atoms and rearranging the molecules in a new order. Hector popping his eye out, it's like his party trick to show that he's mastered advanced physics.'

'Right,' mumbled Dude feeling none the wiser.

'Well, go on then,' said Hector, popping his eye back in, 'In you go.'

Dude looked at the back of Betty's head and wondered exactly *how* to get in.

'Through the ear-hole, lad,' said Hector, then chuckled. 'Don't go trying the nose like some idiots do. First one to do it was back in the sixteenth century. Got stuck up there for days. Hence the term 'bogey' when something ucky's stuck in your nose. So go on, don't hang about.'

'Grey, *help* me,' said Dude. 'I don't know what to do.'

'It's all down to using your will again, like you do when you want to pick things up or touch someone, you make your hand feel solid. You will it, right?'

'Right,' said Dude.

'OK,' said Grey. 'Well, this time, you don't want to think yourself solid, oh no, that would be a major disaster. No, this time, you need to will yourself to be like gas ...'

'*Whadt*?' exclaimed Dude.

'Bear with me, man,' said Grey. 'Matter is made up of atoms all linked together. Gas is made up of atoms all separate and doing their own thing. With me so far?'

'Sort of,' said Dude.

'OK. So all the atoms, this time, instead of holding hands and legs, you imagine them letting go, doing their own thing as individual octopuses, then imagine them shrinking, going tiny, tinier, miniscule, then see them forming a line, one after the other – and off they go straight into Betty's ear. Think it and it will happen. Visualise yourself as a tiny Dude, like a Dude bug...'

'A doodlebug? But that's a bomb!' said Dude.

'Concentrate, Dude,' said Grey. 'Not doodlebug, oh god no, you'd blow Bettie sky high if you imagined you were a doodlebug. No. A *Dude* bug. Concentrate. Imagine the octopuses letting go of hands and legs, then see them shrinking to tiny. Then march them into the ear-hole and, once inside, let go of the visualisation and think yourself back to your normal size.'

Dude looked very worried. 'But how can we both fit in? Me and Betty?'

'It will be all right, honest, trust me,' said Grey. 'You're not made up of matter remember? You're as insubstantial as a shadow. A human can stand next to a shadow and it doesn't squash them out does it? So chill. You'll be all right. And just think yourself tiny to get out again.'

Dude looked back at Betty and recoiled. Her ear didn't look too savoury. It was hairy and looked as if she hadn't cleaned it in weeks.

'But why the ear-hole?' asked Dude.

'Auntie Betty is clairaudient as well as clairvoyant,' said Grey. 'See, there are different types of psychics. Clairvoyants who see ghosts, clairsentients who sense ghosts and clairaudients who hear ghosts. It's the same with all the audients. Their ear-hole is the portal between them and the ghost world. Go on. Stop wasting time.'

Dude still didn't fancy slipping down a waxy lughole,

portal or not. However, before he could make a move, he was shoved aside. It was Bella.

'When did you get here?' asked Dude.

'Minute ago and I've got a few things to say to Tara before you,' she said. And before he knew it, she'd gone, straight down Auntie B's ear.

Dude had to act fast when he heard Bella's voice come through Betty.

'So, Tara,' she began. 'I just want to say, stay away from Dude. He's my boyfriend now.'

Tara went white and clutched Liam's hand.

Dude forced his mind to focus. *Small octopes all letting go of their neighbours' hands and legs*, he thought, *small individual octopes*, and to his amazement, he found himself shrinking.

In a flash, Dude climbed onto Bettie's shoulder, held his nose and dived. Straight down her lughole with his eyes shut tight. His landing felt soft and squashy, as he pushed Bella aside. He let go of his visualisation to be tiny and felt himself expanding again. He opened his eyes and found himself looking out of Auntie Betty's right eye at the room and Tara.

'Curiouser and curiouser,' he said. 'Hey, Tara, it's me...'

'No it's not,' said Bella, pushing him aside again. 'It's me.'

Betty started to shake.

'Oi. Stop larking about in there or I'll have you,' boomed Hector's voice down the ear-hole.

Bella and Dude continued shoving.

'You get out,' said Dude.

'No, I was here first,' said Bella, giving him a good pinch for emphasis.

'It was my turn,' objected Dude. 'Hector said.'

Betty's body rocked back and forth whilst Tara and the others in the room looked on in horror.

'I'm getting out of here,' she said to Liam, as Aunty B's eyeballs began revolving in different directions. 'This is way too spooky.'

'*No*,' called Dude. 'Don't go.'

'No, don't go,' implored Liam. 'Can't you tell that's Dude?'

'Yes, yes Tara, clear off,' called Bella.

'I … I thought for a moment I heard him,' said Tara, 'but no way that last voice was Dude. It was too high-pitched.'

It was starting to feel uncomfortable inside Betty's head as Dude was shoved aside once again. He was pressing up against something big and spongy and he had an awful feeling that it was Aunty B's brain. Bella had taken up prime position but as it was so tight in there, it was causing Betty's tongue to protrude, and the live people on the seats started to look seriously worried.

'Out *now*,' yelled Hector. 'It's not big enough for the two of you in there. You'll do some damage. You. Bella Ghostie, leave the lad alone or you'll have me to deal with.'

'Look, Bella,' said Dude. 'We don't have time for this. Clear off.'

'No,' she said. 'Shan't.'

'Bella if you don't shift yourself and let me talk to Tara then I swear I will ignore you for the rest of my after life, and I will as well. And think about why we're doing this. We're trying to reach Tara to help, help the ghost world, or have you forgotten that we're on a serious mission here? You said you were a fan but you've caused me nothing but trouble …'

'No one *ever* understands me,' said Bella. 'It's not fair.' And then she was gone.

Back in the room, Tara was making for the door.

'Tara, Tara. It's me. Dude. *Tara.*'

Tara looked confused. 'Now, that *does* sound like Dude,' she said.

'Come and sit back down,' said Liam. 'Give him a chance.'

'Don't be scared, love,' said one of the ladies on the seats. 'Just ask him something that no one else could ever know.'

Tara sat down and looked thoughtful. 'OK,' she said. 'What was it Dude always used to say before a gig?'

'Allegiance to the heart,' cried Dude.

Tara's eyes filled with tears. She looked at Liam. 'It *is* Dude isn't it? Oh*migod*, Dude, are you OK?'

'Bit cramped in here,' he laughed. 'But yeah, I'm OK. And if you're not scared and you will to hear me, then you can. That's all it takes – that you will it and you're not frightened. Then I can get out of here.'

'I can even see him,' said Liam. 'Maybe you will be able to as well.'

Tara looked back at Aunty B. 'I won't be scared, Dude,' she said. 'Promise. Please, please come on out. I *do* want to see you. Allegiance to the heart.'

Jack's wife dabbed a tear from her eye. 'Ooh, I love a nice romance,' she said, as all the live people and the ghosts in the queue behind Auntie B cheered.

Fourteen

Dude was overjoyed. Once Tara had got over her fear, not only could she hear him but she could also see him. He showed her all his new tricks, floating six feet up in the air, making himself go small then normal again, walking through doors, and sliding through walls. He soon filled her in on his new life and his new friends, and explained that if she wasn't afraid then she'd be able to see them as well. She only had to will it. Tara was so happy to be with Dude again, she soon caught on and like Liam, found that she could see and hear Grey easily. Grey introduced himself and soon joined in the antics, trying to impress her with his double back-flips and triple somersaults.

'It's amazing,' she said, putting her hand through Dude's shoulder. 'It's like you're here but you're not.'

'Yeah. It's the new look,' he said, strutting down the road outside Auntie Betty's like a supermodel on a catwalk. 'Transparent is the new black. Anyone who's anyone is wearing it.'

Tara giggled, then launched into all the questions that Dude had when he first discovered he was a ghost. 'But what now? Where do you live? With your parents? Can they see you? Do you need to eat? Do you wash? Do you sleep?'

'Why don't we show you where we live?' suggested Grey. 'That way you can see for yourself.'

'Will there be other ghosts there?'

'Bogus – and he's cool. We all live at his gran's house,' said Dude.

'I've met her,' said Liam. 'She's still alive. She's really nice.'

Tara looked unsure. 'Will that weird girl ghost be there? She doesn't like me.'

'You mean Bella?' said Dude. 'She does live there as well, but I'm sure she'll behave now. Come on. You'll like it back at the house. I've got my own room and everything. Just will to see Bogus and Bella and you will.'

Mrs Riley was asleep on the sofa in the living-room when they arrived home an hour later.

'Ooh, another one,' she said, as Dude introduced Tara to her. 'It's getting to be like a railway station in here with all the comings and goings. Pleased to meet you pet. Now you all go up while I watch the telly.' And with that, she settled herself back down and promptly fell asleep again.

The small group trooped up the stairs and into Bogus's room where, as usual, he was bent over the computer. He glanced up, did a double-take, then shifted awkwardly at his desk.

'Hey, Bogus,' said Dude. 'This is my girlfriend Tara. Just will to see him, Tara. He's cool.'

Tara stepped forward and smiled. 'Hi, Bogus. I hear that you're the brains behind this operation.'

Bogus shrugged his shoulders and looked down at the floor. 'Um, yeah, nihi, erghhh. Yeah.'

What's wrong with him? thought Dude. *He's acting really weird.* He glanced back at Bogus who stole a furtive look at Tara from behind his glasses. Then Dude got it. Bogus was shy of beautiful girls. And Tara was a stunner. Bogus had simply lost his tongue. It looked as though Tara had realised this, as she was making an extra effort to put Bogus at ease.

'Dude's filled me in on everything. He tells me that this guy Sid has been causing trouble,' she said. 'Can you show me how?'

With that, Bogus was away, showing off in his own manner. He gave Tara the demonstration that Dude had seen only days before. Dude felt chuffed to see his girlfriend make such an impression, as Bogus bent over backwards to make sure that she understood how ghosts were scanned in then printed out, how the code could be corrupted and how he fixed it.

'Oh, you are clever,' she said, when he'd finished.

Bogus grinned and his white colour began to glow softly pink, right to the end of his ears.

When a beep announced that there was an e-mail, he turned back to his computer and opened it. His face fell. 'It's from Sid,' he groaned.

'What, already?' asked Dude. He leant over Bogus's shoulder and read the e-mail. '"I'm back on line you losers. Get ready for some fun." Oh pants! Now what?'

Bogus started hitting buttons frantically. 'Bella's in there. We've got to her out before it's too late.'

'The *fool*,' said Grey. 'She *knew* it was dangerous to go in at the moment. Why did she do something so stupid?'

Bogus shrugged. 'Came back here with a right strop on. Something about no one ever appreciating her. Says everyone always ignores her and what she has to say. She dived straight in and said she was going to hang out with people who understand her from now on.'

'Chat-room,' said Grey and Dude together.

Seconds later, Bogus found her in Goth City and when he told her that Sid was back on line, she came out onto the desk top double-quick.

When Bogus printed her out, the Dead Dudes all

118

gasped in horror.

'What?' she said, looking round and frowning on seeing Tara. 'What's *she* doing here?'

Tara looked the other way. 'What are you all looking at?' she asked Bogus, Dude, and Grey.

'Bella,' said Dude. 'Can't you see her? You must be able to see her. Bella, what happened?'

'What do you mean? Why are you all staring at me?' asked Bella.

The Dead Dudes shifted nervously. Bella had turned bright green and had an extra arm.

Finally Bogus pointed at the third arm.

'Ohmigod,' she cried looking down. 'And I'm *green*. Bogus, *DO* something.'

'This has to be Sid's doing,' said Bogus. 'He's clearly come up with some kind of new virus that can get through my anti-Sid virus software. He must know he can't delete the ghost code any longer so he's come up with a new devious plan – to *add* elements to ghost codes. Yeah, Sid, most amusing. Not.'

'Well, at least he couldn't wipe her out,' said Grey.

'Bogus please, *do* something,' Bella implored, as her third arm started pulling her hair.

'I can't,' stuttered Bogus. 'At least I could if you were on the screen but we can't risk you going back in. Not now, there's no telling what else Sid could do to you.'

The dudes looked at Tara.

'What? Why you all looking at me?' she asked. 'I can't see anyone.'

'Bella's come back,' said Liam. 'You must be able to see her if you can see the others.'

'Well, maybe green is a fitting colour for her seeing as she's so full of envy,' said Tara, then looked sheepish as she realised that she'd let on that she could see Bella.

Dude sighed. *Girls* he thought. He knew exactly what Tara was up to. Pretending that Bella was invisible just to annoy her. He had to think of a way to get her to help them without letting her jealousy get in the way.

'That could happen to me,' he said. 'Sid could do that to me and possibly worse if you don't help, Tara. He may even wipe me out completely and then I'd never be able to see or talk to you again.' He put on his best little boy lost look. 'Please help. We need you.'

Tara looked from ghost to ghost. The ghosts looked imploringly back at her.

'Well, OK, you all look like you *do* need help,' she said finally. 'Especially the Queen of Green.'

'You want me to *what?*' said Tara, after Bogus explained what needed to be done. 'You want me to go and pretend that I fancy some spotty creep. No *way*. Hey, I've got a reputation to keep up. You must be out of your heads. Oh. Sorry ... you are.'

'Oh, don't be like that Tara,' pleaded Dude. 'You said you would. And we'll be right there with you. Nothing can go wrong.' Dude noticed that, thankfully, Liam was keeping very quiet about the last little episode round at Sid's.

'Told you she'd be useless,' Bella laughed. 'Reputation, huh? And I suppose having a ghost for a boyfriend's mega cool?'

This obviously irked Tara. 'Well, he's not any ordinary ghost is he? He's Dude. And I'm *not* useless. At least I'm not green. In fact, count me in boys.'

'Right,' said Bogus. 'This is the plan. Dude, Grey, you go with Tara. Might be too dangerous for you to actually go into the room again. Best wait outside until her and Sid are safely upstairs, then slip up there and wait on the landing. Bella you'll stay here with me, won't you?'

'Yeah, whatever,' said Bella, desperately trying to regain her cool despite being a nasty shade of boiled cabbage. 'No way I'm going out like *this*.'

'Good,' continued Bogus. 'Tara, while you distract Sid, Bella can go back on screen and I can fix her. Tara, if you want help, say you need the bathroom and Dude will meet you there. Everyone got it?'

Everyone nodded. 'Got it, Bogus.'

'OK, Mr Grey, you're with me,' said Dude. 'Miss Green you stay here with Mr Silver. Let's go to work.'

Fifteen

Sid's jaw almost hit the floor when he saw a blonde babe in a pink mini-dress standing at his door half an hour later.

'Hi. I'm Tara Jacobs,' she said, batting her long eyelashes at him.

'Well, hi there, baby doll,' said Sid, going into slimeball routine. 'So what can I do for you?'

'I'd er, like to ask you a favour,' pouted Tara.

'A favour, eh? OK. Come in.' He quickly checked the landing then pointed upstairs. 'Go on up. We can probably talk more comfortably in my room. You first.'

Tara went up the stairs followed by Sid, who punched the air behind her gleefully. A moment later, Dude and Grey glided up and hovered on the landing.

'Now what can I do for you?' asked Sid, shutting his bedroom door.

'Well I've heard so much about you,' purred Tara, trying not to reel at the stink coming from a pile of dirty laundry in the corner. 'I've been told that you're the man to talk to when it comes to ... ghosts.'

Dude slid his hand through the bedroom door and gave her the thumbs up so that she knew that he was there and not to worry.

'Ghosts?' asked Sid, suddenly looking suspicious. 'You don't know a kid called Liam do you?'

Tara shook her head. 'No, why?'

'Had a bit of trouble with him,' he said, rubbing his

arm. 'Brought a load of ghosts here, not long ago. Got to be careful.'

'*Real* ghosts? It must have been *awful* for you,' said Tara. 'What happened?'

'Oh, no problem. I sorted him and his spook mates. No, he won't be back here in a hurry.'

'Really,' said Tara, trying not to smile, as Dude stuck a leg through the door and wiggled his foot. 'You're *very* brave to do this sort of work.'

Sid's chest swelled. He was clearly a sucker for flattery. 'Yeah, you better believe it. So you got a ghost you need me to get rid of?'

Tara shook her head. 'Gosh, no. Nothing that drastic. I'm doing an article for the school magazine about ghosts and everyone said that you'd done one last year. Only one man to talk to, everyone said. Sid Wiper. He knows everything about ghosts.'

Sid smirked happily. He motioned her to sit on the bed next to him. 'You've come to the right place and better sit close, angel, because I can tell you, ghosts are very, *very* frightening.'

'Um, yeah, right, *terrifying* in fact,' said Tara, desperately trying to keep a straight face as Dude and Grey stuck their bottoms through the door and mooned at Sid.

'So, fire away' said Sid. 'What do you want to know?'

Tara crossed her legs and got out her note-pad. 'Well, what got you started?'

'Had a close escape when I was younger,' said Sid. 'Then I read all I could about them, saw all the movies, I realised that it was something I had to do. I'm here to fight the evil forces that exist beyond the grave.'

At this point, Dude and Grey stuck their heads through the door and did their most frightening faces. Dude made

123

his eyes go cross-eyed, and Grey stuck his tongue out and waggled it.

'What, like Buffy the Vampire Slayer?' asked Tara, trying not to laugh.

'Yeah,' said Sid. 'Only I'm the ghost slayer.'

'So how do you do it?' she asked.

Sid tapped the side of his nose. 'Ah. That's for me to know,' then he leant close to her, 'And you to find out.'

'Fascinating,' she said, trying not to recoil at the proximity of him. 'Please tell me.'

Sid thought for a minute. 'OK, but this is between me and you and not for publication. Deal?'

'Our little secret,' said Tara, giving him her most brilliant smile. 'I promise.'

'A lot of it's done on computer,' he said, taking her hand in his sweaty palm. 'Simple really. See, ghosts like to surf the Net. Find the code element common to all ghosts and it's a synch. All you need to do is mess about with symbols on the code and they're either gone or ... how can I put it? Heh, heh, let's just say, altered.'

'It sounds so complicated,' said Tara, slipping her hand out of his. 'You must be *very* clever. But do all ghosts surf the Net?'

Sid's face clouded. 'Most of them. I'm still trying to work out how to wipe out the others.'

'But surely not all ghosts are bad, Sid,' she said. 'Have you ever tried giving them a chance? Maybe try to communicate properly?'

'Are you out of your mind? Ghosts are the vermin of the after-life. They must be terminated. And I am the Terminator. Let me show you how. It's a real buzz. Want to see how it's done?' he asked, indicating his computer.

Dude shoved his face through the door. 'Quick, Tara.

124

Bella will be on-line while Bogus tries to fix her. Quick. Distract him.'

'Um, Sid. This is *soo* fascinating but do you mind if I use the bathroom before you start?' she asked.

'Sure,' said Sid, pointing at the door. 'Down the corridor, first on the left. Hurry back, won't you?'

'Can't wait,' she muttered to herself as she headed for the door.

Once on the landing, she pulled a disgusted face then raced down the corridor and into the bathroom. It smelt as bad as Sid's bedroom and was filthy, with stray hairs and slimy soap on every surface.

'Ewww,' she said, as Dude and Grey slipped through the door to join her. 'That boy is creepier than any ghost could ever be. And this place stinks.'

'Tell me about it,' said Dude, holding his nose and putting the toilet-lid down. 'I guess just because people have money, doesn't mean they're hygienic.'

'Or have taste,' said Grey, looking at the enormous gold taps on the pink bathtub.

'What are we going to do?' asked Dude.

Tara looked around helplessly. 'Don't know. Bogus didn't have a plan beyond us getting here. What *shall* we do?'

Suddenly, there was a knock on the door. 'Who are you talking to in there?' demanded Sid.

'Shhh,' said Grey. 'Mustn't let him know we're here.'

'Um, singing,' said Tara. 'La la la la laaah. Um, all our family do it in the loo, um, good acoustics ...'

'OK, but I'm waiting,' said Sid.

Grey looked thoughtful. 'I've got a plan,' he whispered. 'Remember how the ghosts spoke through your Auntie Betty?'

125

'Yes,' said Tara.

'How about I speak through you? Like the ghosts did through Auntie B? Tell him that I've come to get him back for his ghostbusting activities. He'll freak, because you're solid and he won't understand how. Then we can threaten him.'

Tara looked doubtful. 'But ...'

'It's too dangerous,' said Dude.

Sid knocked again. 'What are you doing in there? Recording an album. Come *on*. I want to show you how I play with ghosties on my computer.'

'All right,' said Tara. 'It may just work. Auntie Betty told me how to do it when I was a little girl. She said when I grew up I could be a medium. I never believed in all that hocus-pocus until the other day ... so let's give it a go. But Dude, *you* speak through me, not Grey. And Grey, you back us up with a few tricks.'

Dude took a deep breath. 'I don't know ...'

'Bella gets it if we don't,' said Grey. 'And she's all right really. I know she can be trouble sometimes, but she doesn't deserve to be green for the rest of her death. And if we don't stop Sid, it could be us next.'

'Yeah the kid's a *real* sicko. He's got to be stopped,' agreed Tara, as she washed her hands.

Dude nodded and looked at Tara. 'OK. Ready?'

'Ready,' she said, closing her eyes.

Dude took a deep breath, willed himself miniscule then slid down her ear-hole.

'OK, say something,' said Grey.

Dude got the giggles. 'Well, firstly I'd like to say that there's not a lot of mystery left when you've seen the inside of your girlfriend's eyeballs.'

'Can you see me?' asked Grey.

126

'Not yet. It's a bit cramped in here. Not as much room as Auntie Betty. I'm trying to line up with her eye sockets. She's smaller than me. I'm having to look down her nose. Oops. I'll shrink myself a tiny bit and line up the knee-caps. Yep. Hey, I'm really getting the hang of this. Yeah. Here we go. You OK, Tara?'

'I don't think she can speak when you've got the vocal chords,' said Grey. 'You OK, Dude?'

'Yeah. This is amazing. Like wearing clothes. Really heavy clothes. Yo. I'd forgotten how solid these body things were. Right, let's go.'

There was another impatient rap on the door, so Tara opened it and smiled at Sid.

'You sure you weren't talking to someone in there?' he asked.

Tara shook her head and went back into Sid's bedroom. Once he'd followed her in, she kicked the door shut.

She pushed him down into a sitting position, then stood over him and rolled her eyeballs alarmingly.

Dude put on his best scary voice. 'Sid Wiper,' he said. 'Siiiiid Wiiiiiper, I have come to get you.'

Sid went white. He cowered back on his bed and curled up against the wall. 'What's going on? Who's that? Tara, is this a joke? Because I ain't laughing.'

'Who – Wh*ooooo* ha hahh. No joke, mortal. I am he*eee*,' said Dude, frantically searching his mind for some good scary names. Suddenly he remembered the list of teens in the Goth city chat-room. 'Yes. I am he*eee*. Bogeye. Protector of the beyond. Black Sab. Sadsadie…..,'

Grey shook his head. 'No, no,' he gestured. 'Not Sadsadie…'

'Ahem,' continued Dude, 'er, that is I mean… I am Dark Angel, Gothmoth the *Teeeeerrible.*' Then he did a manic high-pitched laugh.

'Oh my god, something's got into the bathroom and possessed you,' cried Sid looking around frantically. 'Who is it? What are you?'

'Prince of Ghoul,' wailed Dude. 'Revenger of the tormented.'

Behind him, Grey was busy making the room safe. He turned off the computer, unplugged it, then whirled the computer cable in the air like a whip.

'What do you want, oh Prince of Ghoul?' whispered a terrified looking Sid, as the cable narrowly missed his ear.

'I want you to leave us aloooooone,' said Dude. 'You must stop all your ghostbusting activities now and foreeeeever or suffer the consequences.'

Sid wasn't going to give in easily, though. He leapt off the bed and reached out for his scanner, but Grey was too quick for him and flicked the cable round his knees tipping him back onto the bed.

'Be still, you of putrid flesh,' cried Dude, as he and Grey held Sid down.

'What *are* you?' screamed Sid. 'You have many hands.'

'Many hands make light work,' said Grey, as he flicked on the light next to the bed and held it over Sid's face, making him blink against the bright glare.

'I am heeeee. Most powerful of ghoooosts,' continued Dude. 'I can take on any form. I have come to right the wrongs of my brothers. Oh … and sisters too. And the next body I come in won't be so nice, in fact, it will be very nasty *indeeeeeeed.*'

Sid lay on the floor shaking. 'Oh, please don't hurt me, please don't hurt me.'

That gave Dude an idea. 'I'm afraid I have no choice.

128

The damage you have done has been … um … dreadful.'

Sid rolled into a ball and rocked back and forth. 'Don't hurt me, don't hurt me,' he moaned.

'If you do not behave in the future,' continued Dude, who was beginning to enjoy himself tremendously by now, 'Your fate will be terrible. I and others like me will be back. We will … we will give you terrible …'

'Boils…' whispered Grey.

'BOILS,' cried Dude. 'Big, throbby, red, white-headed ones. A stonker on the end of your nose. And another on your forehead. You will be laughed off the beach in summer. Sand kicked in your face although … you *will* be in great demand at Christmas – as Rudolf the red-nosed reindeer.'

'*Noooo …*' wailed Sid.

'We will give you buckteeth and make you bald by the time you are 18. No girl will ever look at you except with pity. Haha, hahahahaha.'

'*No,*' cried Sid. 'Please …'

'It's either girls or ghosts,' said Dude. 'You choo-ooooose.'

Sid looked hesitant, so Dude thought he'd better add something else to make sure that the job was well and truly done. 'And we'll shriiiink your wiiiillie. And make it bent. With a haaaair on the end.'

'That's hitting a bit below-the-belt,' chuckled Grey flicking the cable around Sid's head.

'I promise,' whimpered Sid. 'Just go away and I promise I'll never dabble in the ghost world again.'

'Never?' asked Dude.

'Never *ever*,' blubbed Sid.

'And what about on the computer? Will you leave ghosts free to surf?'

Sid nodded.

'Because if you so much as look at a ghost's code again, I'll be back. I'll be waaaatching you. Every day, every niiiight. You will *never* be alone again.'

'I promise, I promise,' sobbed Sid, who by now was a blubbering heap.

'My woooork here is done,' said Dude. 'We shall leave you but remember we will be waaaaatching you. One wrong-doing and my vengeance will be terriiiible.''

Sid nodded from the carpet. 'I'm sorry, I'm sooooorry.'

Grey gave Dude the thumbs up. 'Let's beat it,' he said.

Sixteen

'OK, you can come out now,' said Grey, as they turned the corner away from Sid's street.

'Right,' said Dude, and slid out of Tara's ear.

Tara's body went limp and slumped onto the pavement. A woman with a push-chair stared with concern from the other side of the road and began to come over.

'Holy Moley,' cried Dude. 'What's happened?'

'Dunno,' gasped Grey. 'Quick, get back inside and we'll go to Bardo Street. Bogus may know what to do.'

Dude slid back in double-quick and stood Tara's body up.

'You all right, Miss?' asked the woman.

Dude nodded. 'Fine,' he whispered. 'I'm fine. Just felt a bit faint.'

'You sure?'

Dude nodded again and walked quickly away.

'Oh, *no*,' he said to Grey. 'What if she's gone for ever? I'll never forgive myself. I *thought* it was too risky.'

'Double oh no,' cried Grey pointing down the street. 'Quick. Act natural. Here comes her mate Jenni.'

Dude tried to duck into a doorway but Tara's ankle gave way. 'High-heels,' he moaned. 'How am I supposed to walk in these things?' He attempted to run but too late, Jenni had seen Tara and was walking towards her.

'Hey, Tara,' she said. 'Where've you been?'

'Um, shopping,' squeaked Dude trying to speak in a girlie voice.

131

Jenni looked closely at Tara. 'You all right? You sound kind of weird.'

Dude coughed. 'Throat bug. That's where I've been. Chemists. Lozenges. Have to go. Feel awful.'

'You poor baby. Want me to walk home with you?'

Dude shook Tara's head. 'No, I'll be fine. Honest.'

He began to walk away when Grey whispered. 'Walk like a girl you dork. You're walking like a rugby player.'

Dude turned back to see Jenni looking anxiously after him. He gave her a wave. 'Fine. Really, fine,' he began to limp. 'Hurt my knee as well.'

He straightened up. *What's my motivation* he thought. *I am a girl. A babe. With a sore knee. Got to get in touch with my feminine side.*

'How am I doing Grey?' he asked as he minced down the road and round a corner.

Grey leant against a wall and cracked up laughing. 'Don't ring us Mrs Dudefire. We'll ring you,' he chuckled.

Ten minutes later and they were back at Bardo Street.

As usual, Mrs Riley was in the kitchen. Bogus and Bella were with her, sitting at the table ready for a hit of an apple-pie that had just come out of the oven.

'Hey you're back to normal,' said Dude, looking at Bella who was back to her usual silvery grey.

Bella looked up. 'Tara, what are you doing here?' she spluttered.

'It's not Tara,' said Dude. 'At least, it *is* Tara but it's really *me*. Dude. I … I …'

'He had to do an 'Auntie Betty' only using Tara's body,' explained Grey. 'But it's Dude inside, believe me. It was the only way to get through to Sid. Long story … Explain later. Anyway Bella, back to normal?'

Bella smiled and pointed at Bogus. 'Thanks to our computer whiz, here,' she said. 'He deleted the elements that made me green.'

'Elementary, my dear Watson,' smiled Bogus. 'So how did it go?'

'We've got a problem,' sighed Grey.

'What is it, Grey?' asked Mrs Riley.

'Bit of a mix-up. We had to scare Sid off ghostbusting, so Dude spoke through Tara and now we can't get her back.'

'Oh dear,' said Mrs Riley, shaking her head. 'Oh dear, oh dear, oh dear.'

Dude in the meantime, was eyeing the apple pie. *I wonder* … he thought.

'You want a piece, don't you?' asked Grey.

Dude nodded and cut himself a generous slice. 'Too good an opportunity to miss,' he said and quick as a flash, he'd shoved the pie into his mouth. 'It's worth a try.'

Grey shook his head. 'You'll be able to chew and swallow but it won't be the same, man.'

Grey was right. It was like chewing cardboard. Dude could taste the apples and the pastry but it wasn't anywhere near as good as inhaling. He went over to the bin in the corner and spat the pie out. Then he sat down and joined in the group sniffing.

'Nah, didn't really work. It's weird. It hasn't been long but already I prefer the aroma of things. So much more subtle.'

'Ummmmm,' said the other Dead Dudes as they inhaled the delicate flavours.

'So what are we going to do?' asked Bella.

'Call Auntie Betty,' said Bogus. 'She may be able to tell us.'

'Yeah,' said Grey. 'I've got one of her business cards somewhere. The number will be on there.'

Grey found the card then Mrs Riley picked up the phone and dialled. The Dead Dudes watched anxiously as she filled Auntie Betty in on the problem, then listened and nodded, shook her head, and nodded again.

'What?' asked Dude, when she finally put the phone down. 'What did she say?'

'She says Tara's probably on an astral plane somewhere.'

'That's where people go when they dream,' said Bogus. 'You mean she's asleep?'

Mrs Riley nodded. 'Betty said we need to lay her down comfortably then gently try to wake her.'

'Excellent,' said Dude, getting up. 'I'll take her up to Bogus's room.' Suddenly he felt a cramp deep in Tara's abdomen. 'Oh no, I think her body's ill. No. Oh, no. Oh, *nooo*. She, her, she needs ...' He crossed his legs and bent over.

Grey creased up. 'To use the bathroom. You *are* in a live body Dude. They still need to do that kind of thing.'

Bogus and Bella fell about laughing.

'What am I going to do?' said Dude. 'I can't ... no way ...'

'I'll take her,' said Bella. 'You come out and I'll go in and take her.'

'Can we trust you?' said Bogus.

Bella nodded. 'If it wasn't for her, I'd still be green with three arms. It's the least I can do.'

Dude nodded. 'I trust you, Bella,' he said.

Bella grinned from ear to ear then she and Dude swopped places inside Tara.

Once Bella had been to the bathroom, she went into

134

Bogus's room and lay down on the covers of Bogus's bed. When she had made Tara's body comfortable, Bella slipped out and stood at the end of the bed with the others.

'Well done, Bella,' said Dude. 'You're a good girl.'

Bella smiled shyly. 'Thanks, Dude. Now, how do we wake her?'

'Sing to her Dude,' suggested Grey.

Dude launched into a song as everyone looked on, willing her to wake up. But she just lay there snoring gently.

'Maybe you should wake her with a kiss,' said Bogus. 'Worked in Snow White and the Seven Dwarfs.'

'Good idea,' said Dude, and leant over and pressed his lips against hers. But his lips went straight through, crashing into teeth, her tongue, past her tonsils and into something slimy and grey, then he floated down through the pillow, through the bed, and onto the carpet under the bed, where he landed with a soft thump.

'Yurggh, forgot to put my brake on until the last moment,' he said, crawling out from under the bed and getting up. 'I just snogged her brain.'

Bella cracked up. 'Typical boy. Sees a girl he fancies and his brain goes to mush.'

'And you forgot to make yourself feel solid, didn't you?' asked Bogus.

'Of corpse,' said Dude, slapping his forehead. 'Want me to try again?'

He willed all the atoms in his face to be glued together then bent over again, being careful to put his inner brake on. Just as he was about to press his lips on Tara's, she opened her eyes.

'Arghhh!' she cried.

'*Arghhh!*' he cried.

'I had the weirdest dream,' she said, sitting up. 'I dreamt I had a really bad head cold.'

'That was Prince Dude kissing you,' laughed Grey.

'Oh sorry, Dude,' she said, sadly. 'No offence but snogging ghosts isn't covered in Just 17. I wasn't sure how it would feel.'

'You all right?' asked Dude.

Tara nodded. 'Did it work with Sid?'

'It did,' said Grey. 'Dude was magnificent. The Prince of Ghoul. Gothmoth the terrible.'

'Gothmoth the terrible?' giggled Tara.

'It was enough to scare the living daylights out of Sid,' said Grey. 'He's promised to leave us alone from now on.'

'Hope so,' said Tara. 'But just in case, I'll make sure I clock him every now and then. Warn him that we're still watching him.'

'Excellent,' said Bogus.

'Most excellent,' said Dude. 'And we couldn't have done it without you Tara, we owe you a huge thank you.'

'Yeah, thanks,' said Bogus and Grey who then turned to look at Bella.

'Yeah, Tara,' she said, with a genuine smile. 'Big thank you from me and sorry for being a pain. You're OK.'

Tara smiled. 'Cool,' she said simply.

Tara seemed none the worse for wear considering her experiences, and even forgave Dude for scuffing up her expensive shoes. After Mrs Riley had plied her with apple-pie and custard, the Dead Dudes waved her off.

Dude felt sad as he watched her walk away down the street. To a different life. One where he knew he no longer belonged. He knew he could still visit her, but it wouldn't be the same. She needed to move on.

'So what now?' he asked. 'Task completed. Sid's sorted, so is it time to go up to the next level?'

Bogus shook his head. 'Who knows. Moving on to the next level is like dying in the live people's world. You never know when it's going to happen. It happens to some people when they're young, some people live until they're ancient.'

'So maybe I can hang around with Tara and Liam some more?' asked Dude.

Grey put his arm round him. 'You can still watch over them when they're in need, and even talk to them every now again, but your life is with us now. Best if you try to move on.'

'I guess,' he sighed. 'Just sometimes it's hard to let go.'

'For them too,' said Bella, as she watched Tara walk down to the end of the street then stop and look back with a sad expression on her face.

Seventeen

It was two days later when the Dead Dudes got the summons from Hector.

'We're for it now,' sighed Bogus. 'He only asks to see you in person if he's really angry.'

'It's probably my fault,' said Bella. 'From when I jumped into Aunty B when it was Dude's turn.'

'Nah,' said Grey, shaking his head. 'I reckon it's me he wants to see. He's copped on that I went to the movies and was late meeting Dude when he first passed away.'

Dude looked sheepish. 'Actually I think it may be me who's in for it. Friday afternoon, I took a trip to my old school and freaked out one of my old teachers.' Then he grinned. 'It was good though. Mr Philips, the maths teacher. He never liked me. I floated all his books up onto the ceiling then started writing on the blackboard. You've never seen thirty kids try and get out of a classroom so fast. It was complete mayhem. So sorry, dudes, I reckon it's me that Hector's mad at.'

'Nah. We all visited our old schools when we were first ghosts, didn't we?' asked Grey looking at Bogus who nodded.

'Yeah,' said Bogus. 'Got to have some fun. No, I reckon it's me Hector wants to see.'

'But what have you done?' asked Dude.

'Didn't take Gloria, that new assistant of his, seriously – when she e-mailed asking that we call ghosts mortally challenged from now on. Remember that e-mail?'

The others nodded.

'I sent one back saying we wanted to be called the Dead Dudes instead,' continued Bogus. 'I reckon that's what it's all about.'

'Well, best not keep him waiting,' said Mrs Riley. 'Best get along and see what he wants.'

Hector had asked them to be at the town hall, 4pm prompt, on Sunday. It was a very grand building in a posh square in the middle of town, and had tall marble pillars either side of a double wooden door with highly polished brass knobs. Inside, there were mosaic floors and high carved ceilings. Dude felt very small as he slid in after the others.

'Hector used to work here when he was alive,' said Grey.

'Smells nice,' said Dude, as he sniffed in the smell of the beeswax polish that was used on the wood-panelled walls.

'I feel like I'm going to see the headmaster,' said Grey.

'I hope he doesn't lock us up in here or anything,' said Bogus. 'I've heard that there are dungeons downstairs and there's bound to be some seriously disturbed ghosts hanging about down there if they haven't gone up to the next level yet. You know, all those ones that were kept prisoner and tortured and stuff.'

'Thanks,' said Dude. 'You're making me feel a whole lot better.'

'Well, I told you that ghosts are just like people in life,' said Grey, 'some nice, some weird ... talking of which ...'

A middle-aged ghost with frizzy hair and a long flowery skirt bustled out to meet them.

'Gloria,' whispered Bogus to Dude.

'Hector's waiting for you in there,' she said, and

pointed at two tall glass doors.

Oh dear, thought Dude. *I hope he doesn't split us up or anything. I was just starting to feel settled at Mrs Riley's with my new mates. Or maybe it's time for the next level but I don't think I'm ready yet. I want to hang out on this level a bit longer.*

The Dead Dudes slipped through the doors and found themselves in a large, dimly lit hall with a stage at one end.

'Come,' said a voice from the corner of the room. Dude felt a shiver run down his spine, as he strained to see in the darkness, and there was Hector. He didn't look happy.

'So,' he said, giving them a stern look. 'You're here.'

'Yes, sir,' said Bogus, looking at the floor. 'And we all want to say that we're very sorry and we won't do it again.'

'Do what again?' bellowed Hector.

'Um, any of it,' said Grey who was also looking at the floor. 'Whatever it is that we've done, we won't do it again.'

'You won't will you?' boomed Hector.

'No, sir,' said Dude, Bella, Grey, and Bogus.

'Well, that's a shame,' said Hector, his face suddenly splitting into an enormous grin. Then he gave an ear shattering whistle and from out of nowhere sprang hundreds of ghosts. Out of the floorboards, from behind the velvet curtains on the stage, from behind the tables and chairs that were stacked round the edges of the room. Fat ghosts, thin ghosts, young, old, every shape and size. There were ghosts from different eras, some elegantly dressed Victorian ladies, some Edwardian kids in sailor suits and straw-hats, some that looked exactly like the medieval peasants that Dude remembered from his history books, and some that looked like Ancient Romans. Then to top it all, Auntie Betty, Mrs Riley and some of her friends sprang out from a hiding place.

'How did they get in?' asked Dude.

'My gran works here as a cleaner on Saturday mornings,' said Bogus. 'She's got the keys.'

'Surprise!' they all shouted, as hundreds of balloons were released from a net on the ceiling.

Dude almost fainted with shock, but he didn't have time because, in an instant, four ghosts who looked like rugby players hoisted him up on their shoulders. He looked over at Grey and he was also being carried by a mass of ghostly shoulders. And so was Bella. And Bogus.

'For they are jolly good fellows,' sang the ghosts. 'For they are jolly good fellows ... and so say all of us ... and so say all of us ...'

When the singing had stopped, Hector called for silence. 'Ahem. Attention please. Right, now. We thought we'd have a bit of a do to show our appreciation to you lot at Bardo Street. You stopped Sid Wiper's little antics and once again, our ghost community is safe. So, thank you. Ahem, much appreciated, yes, indeedie-do. Three cheers for Bogus.'

'Hip-hip-hooray,' cried the ghosts.

'Three cheers for Grey.'

'Hip-hip-hooray.'

'Three cheers for Bella.'

'Hip-hip-hooray,' they cried again, whilst some of the younger ghosts wolf-whistled.

'And lastly, of course, thanks to Dude. But also, we wanted an occasion to welcome him into our midst properly. So three cheers for Dude.'

'Hip-hip-hooray.'

After that, there were all sorts of wonderful things to inhale, all laid on courtesy of Mrs Riley, Auntie Betty, and some of her old wrinkly helpers. Grey beamed widely as he surveyed vats of chilli con carne, huge tubs of ice-cream, chocolate mousse, trifle, and strawberry milk shakes with extra strawberry.

Then, everyone got into a long line and did the conga around the room. When they'd done that and were all recovering, some of the older ghosts suggested doing the hokey cokey, so the younger ones stood round the sides of the hall to watch.

'You put your left leg in, you put your left leg out, in out in out shake it all about,' sang the ghosts – and some of them did it. Literally. They threw their left legs into the centre of the circle with gay abandon. Sadly, that put an end to the game as most of them then fell over as they couldn't dance with only one leg.

'Puts a whole new meaning on being legless,' laughed an old ghost, as he sniffed at a can of lager.

'Oh, they look 'armless enough,' said Dude, as the ghosts moved on to singing, 'You put your left arm in, your left arm out.'

Next on the agenda was karaoke and Hector pushed Gloria up on stage to start the songs. She did 'Killing Me Softly,' then Bogus and Bella got up to sing a belting version of 'Staying Alive'. Grey did his theme tune, 'Sing if You're Glad to be Grey,' and everyone joined in with great gusto on the chorus. Jade the Shade was next with a soulful version of 'I'm a Survivor'. Even Mrs Riley got up and did a neat version of 'Cold As Ice'. Then the crowd started chanting for Dude.

'But won't live people going past hear us all in here?'

asked Dude, as the noise level grew.

Bogus shook his head. 'No worries. They often let this room out for parties and weddings and stuff. What's it going to look like if anyone walked in? A bunch of harmless old dears having a bit of a do, that's all. Don't forget no one can see us ghosts. Now get up there. Hector's calling you.'

Dude got up onto the stage and went over to the microphone. 'I'd just like to say thank you for this wonderful party,' he said. 'As you know I'm new to this world, having recently become mortally challenged.' He flashed a grin at Gloria who blushed to the tips of her ears. 'As you know I was in a band and, in fact, it was while doing a gig that I passed away. Put a whole new meaning to the phrase to die on stage, I can tell you.'

The ghosts laughed and cheered. Then Hector got up to join Dude on stage. 'I don't think we'll be having karaoke from you, my lad,' he said, then whipped out from behind the curtain a large, black, oblong case and handed it to Dude. 'To show our appreciation. Um, er, rock on, as they say.'

Dude just held it for a moment. He knew what it contained and felt really choked up by the gesture.

'Go on, open it,' shouted someone in the crowd.

Dude slowly opened the case and took out a stunning white and gold electric guitar. 'Whoaa!' He beamed as he realised it was a Fender Stratacaster.

Hector gestured to a ghost off-stage and the curtain was pulled back to reveal a stack of Marshall amps. Dude slung the guitar over his shoulder and plugged in.

'Dude, Dude,' chanted the audience.

'Well there's only one song I feel is appropriate at a time like this,' he said, and went into a rock version of 'I

143

Ain't Got No body.'

The ghosts roared with laughter then sang along at the tops of their voices. They hooted and cheered, then danced and danced like there was no tomorrow.